D0053958

# Tom Cringle

## The Pirate and the Patriot

by Gerald Hausman

illustrated by Tad Hills

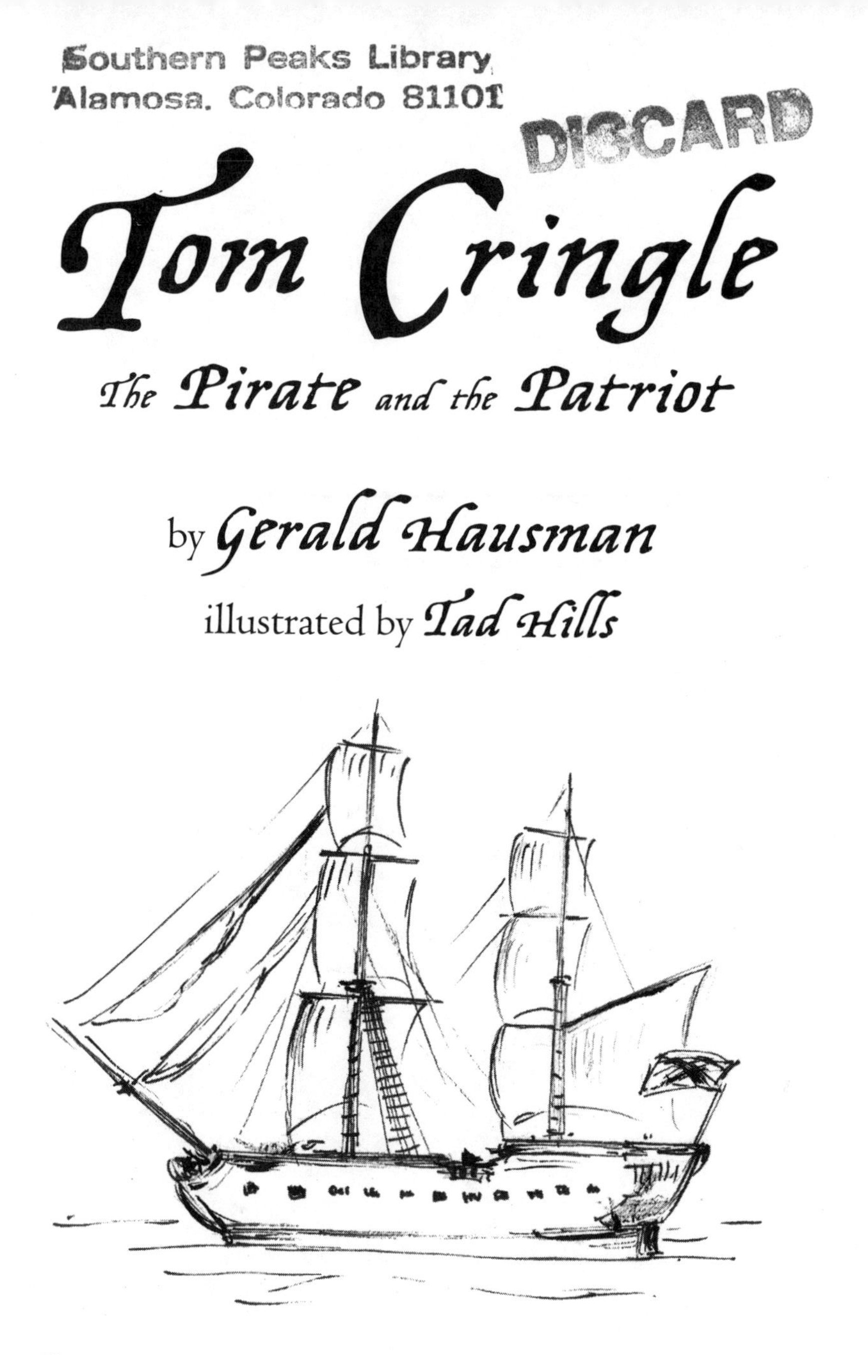



SIMON & SCHUSTER BOOKS FOR YOUNG READERS
New York London Toronto Sydney Singapore

## *Also by Gerald Hausman*

Tom Cringle: Battle on the High Seas

Dogs of Myth

Cats of Myth

SIMON & SCHUSTER BOOKS FOR YOUNG READERS
An imprint of Simon & Schuster Children's Publishing Division
1230 Avenue of the Americas, New York, New York 10020



Book design by Paula Winicur
The text for this book is set in Centaur.
Printed in the United States of America
2 4 6 8 10 9 7 5 3 1

Library of Congress Cataloging-in-Publication Data
Hausman, Gerald.
Tom Cringle : the pirate and the patriot / by Gerald Hausman.
p. cm.
Sequel to: Tom Cringle, battle on the high seas.
Summary: In 1813, a fourteen-year-old British navy lieutenant records in his logbook a perilous journey as he and his men attempt to return a group of slaves to the Jamaican plantation from which pirates stole them; pirates who are determined to reclaim their booty.

ISBN 0-689-82811-X
[1. Jamaica—History—19th century—Juvenile fiction.
[1. Jamaica—History—19th century—Fiction. 2. Pirates—Fiction. 3. Slaves—Fiction.
4. Great Britain—History, Naval—19th century—Fiction. 5. Diaries—Fiction. 6. Sea stories] I. Title.

PZ7.H2883 Tp 2001
[Fic]—dc21
2001017007

*June 5, 1813*
*Onboard the Kraaken, somewhere between Jamaica and Morro Castle, Cuba*

I suppose the thing I am best at is staying alive.

That is, with the help of my great friend Sneezer, a big black Newfoundland dog. The two of us are assigned to the brig the *Kraaken.* Our orders? To capture slavers off the coast of Cuba.

Hard to believe that scarcely one year ago I nearly died there whilst desperately trying to save the notorious pirate Obediah Glasgow. This I survived, too—but he didn't.

In return for capturing Obediah, the Navy raised me up in rank. Me . . . a lad of fourteen, and but five two, and one hundred pounds when wet. So here I'm promoted for capturing my good friend Obediah.

Well, he died by drowning—slipping through my hand—before he could ever be hanged.

And now I'm a hero and an officer, albeit a puny one, and all because I *almost* caught a man destined for the gallows. For better or worse, this curious episode did forge me up into something of "a man of consequence," as my mates like to put it. Yet, beware of vanity, it sayeth in the Bible; these same fellows, well-wishers all, are now more than a little jealous, so I have to watch my step coming and going, and I place my faith solely in such true friends as Peter Mangrove, the African pilot, who has worked his way out from slavery. A likelier candidate for best friend there never was, unless it's Sneezer. Too, there's Tim, my cabin boy, who has the job I had but one year ago.

Well, if you should wonder—I started out wanting to be a sailor. I desired a little coin in pocket and nothing that life doesn't yield as a matter of course; and nothing yielded without hard work. For it was my dear father who said, *You git nuthin' fer nuthin' in this world, lad.* He also said, *Do nothing so poorly as to shame your family.*

Anyway, he was a salty fellow, a sailing man, and I always wanted to be like him, God rest his soul, but Lord knows I never wanted to shame him, or die as he did in a cold trough in the North Atlantic brine.

Sometimes I can scarce believe the deeds duly recorded by my own trembly hand in this logbook of mine. But there's ample proof of pages, not to mention my scattered tears. And even some drops of blood—all proof that I'm both a sailor and a writer; well, a scribe, at any rate.

Once, I recall that after a certain battle at sea, my bookshelf gave way—the whole affair having been split in twain by a round of shot that also shattered my cabin. Down come my logbooks, all carefully bound and marked across the cover, THOMAS CRINGLE, HIS LOGBOOK.

And along comes the gray scowl-face of Mr. Jenkins, the chief lookout, with great alarm, asking me what the jiminy

this log business is about and why I am in my hammock while the shot is rattling tween-decks. Wiping the gunpowder off his face, he asks, "What in the deuce are these?"

"My logs," say I.

"Your what?" His face flushes with contempt. This man hates me from the first, and even now I don't know the full reason why.

"My private journals," I squeak back.

"I will have a turn at them, one day," he remarks venomously, "and if I find a single sour phrase, I shall toss the lot overboard."

They say one man who loathes you is the equal of ten who sing your praises—this is especially true on the deck of a ship outfitted for battle. Well, this Jenkins, my own British countryman, took such a dislike to me, he even tried to kill me—more of that later. "Hadn't you better have your wound dressed, Mr. Jenkins?" I ask, as he is on all fours, bleeding all over my logbooks.

"All right, you little worm," he rasps, getting up and going over to our mess table, which serves as Mr. Jigmaree's surgeon bench, and he bleeds all over that, too.

Some weeks later, with his wounds healed, Mr. Jenkins does me the dubious honor of reading my logbooks, after which he calls me That-Pestilent-Scamp-Cringle-Who-Sleight-of-Hands-Us-Down-to-Posterity. In front of all, he reads my lines aloud—in the meanest of mockery. And believe you me, the men laughed all the more on my account.

And I think they still do, though now I have rank.

*Some hours later on the main . . .*

So far, nothing but fine weather. Wind at east-southeast for a good little while, then a blow from the northwest. This is when I descry a ship's sail on the southeast quarter, and immediately, as fast as I can give the order, we make sail and give chase.

A little after this, Captain Smythe comes on deck.

"We're still on course and in pursuit," I tell him.

"After what—a slaver?"

"Couldn't tell, sir. Wouldn't be surprised, by the way she was tacking to the wind. Slaver or smuggler—or both."

"Aye, keep an eye peeled for her. I have an important letter to write." Then he goes abruptly off, walking a little unsteadily, I think.

For the rest of the day the weather continues roughish, but we do manage to come in sight of that mystery sail. The men are fagged enough, by day's end. As night falls I find myself still on deck, having twice gone to the maintop to spy on the distant sail. I'm as tired as day-old dough when, heading down to eat at last, I jam my left foot in the grating and capsize on my nose.

I curse my bad luck and get to my feet—only to feel them crumple under me. Down I go again like a puppet of wood. When I open my eyes, I find my head resting on a coil of rope, so that my whole head is hanging down within it. Has anyone seen me? I hope not. (If I didn't know that Jenkins was dead, I'd have thought he tripped me.) But here is Sneezer licking me awake, letting me know I am all right. I can only hope that no one saw me take my spill. That no one's belowdecks, laughing at my foolishness—and so I go to eat a well-earned meal, where, thankfully, all are staring into their grog and no one even sees me enter.

*This same wearisome night . . .*

I do as I desire: swallow some grog and turn in. But I'm barely in my hammock above an hour when the drum sounds. Sneezer, who always sleeps beneath my bed, is up and barking as I bundle myself out on the cold, wet deck. And there's the ship—the one we're chasing—right ahead of us and carrying all sail.

Captain Smythe is at work on the fo'c'sle with his night glass. The whole crew's stationed in dark clusters round the guns at quarters. "It's a man-of-war, sir," I hear Mr. Yerk avow.

"She bears the particular stamp of the *Hornet,* I daresay," says the captain.

"Why do you think so, sir?"

"The shortness of her lower masts and the squareness of her yards," Captain Smythe replies.

Then, at that very moment, a whole cloud of studding sails is blown from the yards, and she starts shying off from us and bores up dead before the wind. I join the men in the fo'c'sle, where Captain Smythe, snuffing from his sleeve box, asks, "What think you, Tom?"

At length we get within gunshot.

"Clap the hatches," I tell the men. I pass the word, and our gunner, Mr. Catwell, a round man in a striped jersey, soft afoot and quiet voiced, primes his cannon. Zingo! We have shots flying over and over her.

"No doubt, she's a privateer," I tell Captain Smythe while both of us stand watch on the fo'c'sle. "Put your eye to this," he says, passing me the glass. We're close under her lee quarter, she's not fired a shot, and there's not a man on deck. "Not another Dutchman," I say, sighing, to the captain, meaning, of course, another one of those ghost ships of the night.

The weather—our real enemy—begins to sour again. Shortly thereafter it seems the brig is amongst the breakers. The gale comes on in earnest, spitting in our faces. As we look on, helpless, our prize starts to pull away a little. I'm all over the deck trying to help fit us for foul weather, while Mr. Catwell and Mr. Nedrick and company are struggling in the pitching to clamp down the big guns.

In the sudden blow, the swag of the enemy bumps us. We fetch stern away but run afoul of her. Suddenly, in the heavy sea our stern grinds against the enemy ship's high quarter.

And then all hell breaks loose.

Our mainboom—tangling with the enemy's masts—cracks. Then our ship's mizzen channel begins to make this horrible sawing sound.

I'm running to and fro trying to lash ropes down, and Sneezer's at my heel snapping at them, too. My old friend Peter Mangrove's at my side, and men are shouting and swearing, and the rigging is cracking. Our ship and the enemy vessel are crashing into each other, and it looks as though she'll sink us—or we'll sink her. The damage being equal to each. Then Captain Smythe hollers, "Mind the word of command, men!" He's still got it in him, you see. He can holler over the groan of the gale, "Brace round the foreyard! Round with it—set the jib—that's it—fore-topmast—staysail—haul!"

Whilst he's battening us down, the enemy ship's plunging and pulling a little wide, all snowy with foam.

We clear her then—maybe only by inches—and she slips free; and so do we. By and by, we drop anchor somewhere off the San Pedros Cays.

But the strange thing is, and I shan't forget it—how the enemy that half dismasted us hadn't shown a single face. Tell you the truth, I saw no one on deck, not one soul.

### *June 6*
### *The next night, off the San Pedros Cays*

So here we ride with three anchors ahead, in a little lee. It always chases the willies for me, when I see land, any land, even a bit of sandspit like these bare bones here tween Jamaica and Cuba. This night as our carpenters work on repairs, the sky clears. The stars shine sharp. Not a shred of cloud raking across the moon's clear face.

I'm on night watch again. Sneezer, and Peter, and me. Nothing to do but bear up and keep the eyes open. Below the fo'c'sle the men burn their midnight flares whilst doing repairs. "Devil take we," Peter says. "In me mind, 'twas him dat 'range for us to get sweep by dat ghost ship!"

I chuckle, rubbing the top of Sneezer's tousled black head. "Captain saved the day—and I hardly thought he had it in him, the way he's been rumming of late."

"Him a captain, trew and trew," Peter says. In the distance, the hoarse thunder of the breakers on the beach.

Amidst the hammering and sawing and boiling of pitch and tar, I wonder what it is that makes a captain. It's not just orders and it's not just guts. A little of each; a lot of knowledge. Even drunk, Captain would've known which sails to tie and which to free. His cutting and tying of sails saved us in the stretch. Would I ever be able to do such a quick-witted thing?

*June 7*
*The following day . . .*

We are within pistol shot of Morro Castle, Cuba, coming in on the choppy, churning channel, which is not fifty yards across. Looking down into the water, I see a sunken length of crusted chain made fast to a rock on our larboard side. This chain locks off the channel when there is a battle going on, but now they've laid it low to let us through. Still, I can see it quite clearly, lying like a black serpent on the sparkling sand down below.

Overhead, I hear the loud clap of the golden flag of Spain at the water battery of the castle. The flag casts its large folds abroad on the breeze, and this undulating movement entrances my eye. Then, all of a sudden, just as I'm imagining that things are going smoothly, I feel a wee crunch on the starboard side of the ship, and the land wind checks off and very nearly hoves us broadside on the rocks below Morro Castle.

And things were going so smoothly!

Here, at the castle's webbed foot, I hear thunder break from the swells that flash up, hugely and unpredictably, all round us. What let in all that loose water, I wonder? But I know: It is the tide and the time of day, and who knows what else; it is, indeed, the sea, and she does what she pleases, whenever she pleases, and we men take no comfort in her playfulness, especially now with a whole ship at stake.

"Let go de anchor," Peter sings.

No sooner said than done.

"All gone, sir," cries the boatswain from the fo'c'sle.

However, just as he says this, I am nearly thrown to the deck by one, two, three mammoth crunches! All astern. "The bay has teeth," I grumble under my breath, getting a good grip on the fo'c'sle rail. "Peter, have you lost your eye?" I ask.

Captain Smythe's hand is friskily darting in and out of his coat, his silver flask winking in the sun. I see the ruby red wine dribbling on his chin as we hove, and heave.

Then Peter yells up to me from a rope stay off the

fo'c'sle. Hanging and looking, fore and aft, he hollers, "Just a scratch, Mr. Cringle. Nuh worry, mon."

Out comes the fiery Irish cook, Halsey, stumbling up from the galley with a tub full of yams. Half-naked, in sawed-off trousers and dirty, swinging nightcap, he falls on all fours just as we get yet another crunch. Yams fly into the air, thumping everywhere on the deck.

Halsey thumps about after them, muttering through his tobacco-stained beard, "Oh, you scurvy-looking tief, Peter Mangrove. Cyan't yuh bring us in to shore without so much wrasslin' an' bone breakin'? Cyan't yuh wait till me yams are in the copper, cookin'?"

The canyon walls of the chasm harbor rise some five hundred feet on either side of us, sharp and precipitous, and Halsey's yams are forgotten as we hear the *Kraaken* grinding in the swells—us going up and down as the tide takes a hard turn into the narrow channel.

Captain Smythe, spitting over the larboard side of the ship, curses at Peter, "She's shoal under the bows, man! Haul the cable up!"

By this he means the water is goodly shallow now, so up with the anchor chain so we can float freely again. Who knows whether, under these peculiar tidal conditions, it is better or worse to do this?

"All done, sir, while you was watching Mr. Halsey."

"And the anchor's all right?" Captain Smythe hardly seems appeased.

"Broke de stock short off by de ring," Peter wails. "Nuh worry, sir, she'll fix up quick-quick."

"See that it does, man."

But now we begin to ease into the sea-creviced canyon. Rock walls on either side, close and sharp and tall, and I watch the pointed masts, rocking, and seeming to be writing like pen points on the puff clouds overhead. There are parrots of all sorts, grawking among the outcrops. I go forward and see, suddenly, hummingbirds of all hues darting among the mastheads.

*Afternoon in the channel . . .*

Tim Billingsley, my cabin boy, reminds me much of myself. He's fresh and eager and he's one of the only ones onboard who take my orders as they come, whether or not Captain Smythe is near at hand to bolster them up, which he often does, unless he is too tipsy.

Anyhow, Tim and I meet and talk often. Whenever I see him, I think the only thing that separates us is the number of deaths, sea wrecks, and sicknesses I've seen in the past year. I confess, I don't mind Tim's looking up to me. But his praise makes me nervous.

I break off talking to Tim when I see a strange tree hanging sideways from the cliff. "Not again," I say, sighing, for the branches are tangling with our main-masthead, the one we've just repaired. Before I can say, "Starboard," Peter scrambles up the rigging to help. I sing out, "Let go the anchor!" and down rattles the chain in a blizzard of bubbles.

Up rigging, our lookout, Mr. Tailtackle, is warbling, "Mr. Cringle, I'm stuck!"

"You're *what?*"

"I'm hung fast like a bloody booby among nightingales!"

The idiot's pants are hooked onto a huge horizontal tree that is hanging off the cliff. You see, even though we've dropped anchor, we're still lurching forward. And that is how fellow Tailtackle got chipped in the seat, so to put it.

"Are you all rummed up, man?"

"Nooooo," he crows. "I'm tummied up—to the sky."

"Peter, unfasten the fool from that deuced tree before Captain Smythe wakes up from his boozy nap."

But even as Peter gets up there and makes a grab for Tailtackle's pants, the ship grinds a little farther into the tree, and there he is, plucked like a spring lamb and swinging merrily, as we—anchor down—pull back and away, leaving him hanging a hundred feet above the channel.

If you think this humorous, consider my position—I am senior officer here. If this numskull falls and kills himself, his death will be on my watch! His life, therefore, is in my hands.

A chunk of the tree snaps off and thunders onto the decks. Huge green leaves rain down the rigging. One teardrop-shaped leaf lands on my head, making some of the men laugh. The seriousness of the situation allows me no levity. I make a bad show of tearing off the leaf and stamping on it—this makes them laugh even harder!

Now the *Kraaken*'s gone astern some more. Tailtackle's stranded.

Along comes Captain Smythe, saying, "Where the devil is he?" His face, fresh from his nap, is dark as octopus ink. He is squinting into the sun and craning his neck. "I've lost sight of the bloody fool . . . where the deuce is he?"

"Hanging by a trouser thread, there, sir." I point up to where the bowing tree is showering leaves, shedding parrots. Splendidly and foolishly, Tailtackle is dangling by his trousers. Sneezer is worrying a stick that fell with Tailtackle's maneuvers.

"Where?" The truth is, Captain Smythe is terribly far-sighted. I ascend the fo'c'sle and sort of escort his eye with my right index finger, until he yells, "By Jove, I see him!"

Peter is now at the topmost point of the mast—close, but still off his quarry by a ways. "No use, Tom," he shouts down.

I nod and wave him back down, and he—one leg and two arms—weaves himself to the deck with the ease of a three-legged spider.

"He's three or four yards off de fore-topsail-yardarm," Peter says. The *Kraaken*'s still dropping astern of him. We look on helplessly as poor, dumb Tailtackle walks on air like a man doing a gallows jig. Desperately, he is trying to touch the yardarm with his toes.

"Drunk?" questions Captain Smythe.

"Tailtackled," I reply.

"Listen me, now," Peter says earnestly. "Mek we trow de line round dat stump yonder, den pull de *Kraaken* back under him."

Meanwhile, Tailtackle gets hold of a wiss, a vine, and tearing his pants off, he starts lowering himself down on the thing.

Ogling, Captain Smythe remarks, "Now he's near a foot of that yardarm."

Peter whispers, "No, mon, dat will be de dead of you!"

I glance at Peter and shrug. "Maybe not."

"Wiss too weak to hold a mon dat fat."

Tailtackle, suddenly seeing the true danger of his situation, and that his life is really imperiled, cries out, "Pay out the warp!" By which he means that we should give him more room so he can jump into the water. Still and all, it is a hundred-foot fall, at best.

"Let the ship swing to anchor! I'll be damned if I want to chance falling onto the deck," Tailtackle hollers.

"God bless the bloody fool," Captain Smythe remarks. Then, "If that vine snaps—it's the end of him. Do you think it'll hold up, Tom?"

I shake my head. "Neither does Sneezer, judging by the way he's dancing in a circle and barking up at Tailtackle."

I'm thinking—my first command, and I've got a man marooned in a tree. Mayhap, I've scuttled him. Sometimes I think this life is nothing more than a game of dice. Just bone dice rolling on the deck.

"Him done for," Peter remarks. But he runs forward and tells the men tying us to the stump to set the *Kraaken* free, which they quickly do. The rope groans, slackens. The ship slides astern. For once, Sneezer stops barking. It's as if he knows something is about to happen.

"Let her swing to anchor and pray she clears his way for a free fall into the water," Captain Smythe commands—to no one, really, since the command's already been given by me. He belches, and I catch a sour wind.

"See clear to pick me up," Tailtackle shouts. He is smiling like a circus performer.

I rue the day I ever laid eyes on the man. But I, too, am silently praying that he lands in clear, deep water. Easing astern of him, the *Kraaken* obeys the anchor, giving Tailtackle more room for flight. He slithers down to the very end of the vine. Then, clamping his legs together, he points his toes downward, steadies himself, and with drawn breath, lets go. His big bum looks all the rounder from my point of view—coming down like a cannonball—and now Sneezer sneezes, followed by some baleful howling.

Let him go Godspeed, I pray, and plummet safely—or else I shall have a wicked bad death on my first command post. In truth, I care not for the man but only for a reputation-saving miracle.

Fortune smiles on me again: The big-bottomed bounder drops quite clear of the ship—instantly transformed from sinking clown to conquering hero as he lands with a hearty cheer from the crew, sending up a spume of spray that wets our cheeks.

*Karoosh!*

He vanishes. A frothy scar on the clear blue canal is all we see of him for a moment, then he bubbles up, cheery as a seal.

"Did you ever see such a clean fall, Tom?" asks Captain Smythe.

"Never—he hit the water like a marlinespike!"

Captain Smythe grimaces, shaking his head. "Still, I fear we've got a curse on us this voyage."

"It seems so, sir."

Yet if this be true, Sneezer cares not a fig for it, for he is all over me with happy licks.

*June 8, 1813*
*Next morning, moored in the Morro Channel*

Well, to tell the truth, things *have* gotten sort of loose and lackadaisy. At mess this morning, Captain Smythe requests an audience with Peter, myself, and Lieutenant Yerk. The great bungler, Tailtackle, is not asked to join us—and for the obvious reason that we're probably going to talk about his recent escapade.

"Tom," says Captain Smythe, straight off the cuff, "I'm not a man to mince words, you know. Yesterday was a debacle." From that, and his scowly eyebrows, I know that he is stone-cold sober.

He rivets an angry, clear blue eye on us. Peter throws me a glance, and winks. Captain Smythe looks down the barrel of his big nose, his white side-whiskers all aboil, his wig on crooked. He's a sight, all right. But he means business. "How many crew does it take to come into Morro Channel?" he asks the three of us.

Mr. Yerk, bald head agleam, pipes up pleasantly: "I'd say, sir, it takes a powerful lot of us, judging from yesterday's performance, which was bollixed all the way in. . . ." He's all aglow with his wisdom.

"Shut your pie hole, Mr. Yerk," snaps the captain. "I was speaking, as they call it, rhetorically. Have you any idea what *that is,* Mr. Yerk?"

The accused shakes his head in confusion, for he thought his contribution to the meeting was going quite well. Now his little beady eyes look dazed and moist. He sallies forth, "Well, it means . . ."

The cabin door opens a crack.

Halsey pops in, says, "Beg your pardon, sir, there's a man overboard, sir."

Captain Smythe scratches his snowy muttonchops. He is sweating like a boiled beet. "Overboard—*how?*"

"Swimming, sir."

"A sea bath—while on duty?" Captain Smythe's eyebrows hitch up a notch, and he starts to spit, checks himself, thinks better of it, swallows.

"It seems so, sir," says Mr. Halsey.

Captain Smythe glances sharply from me to Mr. Yerk, then back again to Mr. Halsey, who's wearing a most unappealing blood-spattered apron.

"Well, out with it, Mr. Halsey, who is it . . . Tailtackle?"

"Tim, the cabin boy, sir."

"Oh, for love of Lucifer . . . well, get on deck, Mr. Cringle, and see no harm comes to the lad."

As I get up, Mr. Halsey rubs his hands on his stained apron. "I dumped some guts in the channel this morning," he confesses.

"Are you *daft,* man?"

"I'm *dreadful* sorry, sir."

"Good Christ, Mr. Cringle, get on the deck and see to the boy's safety. Now!"

When Sneezer and I get there, one of Tim's mates is half over the bows, shouting encouragement to him. In the water, splash-wet, his hair all matted down, he looks joyous as a seal pup.

"Tim," I call out, "you know the standing order of the ship?"

He whirls around, midstroke, smiling. His green eyes dancing, his white-white skin so peculiar pale against the blue green flowing stream of the channel current.

"Sir?"

"Come on, Tim, pull for the cable. Get out of the water now."

"What's wrong with me taking a bath? I swabbed deck all morning."

"Well, I'll tell you what's wrong. First, it's against orders. Second, Halsey's tossed some goat guts in there, and we don't know what fish are in there with you. So get out—I won't tell you again."

A couple men in the rigging look over and yell, "Woooo," and show their very obvious mocking, mawkish pleasure at my tough-sounding officer talk. This gives me a bad feeling all over again, and I sweat under my stiffish bolted collar, and I have half a mind to call them down and make them filch the goat guts out of the channel with a net—but to what purpose? They'd like me the less and mock me the more.

"This water's as safe as a Portsmouth tide pool, Mr. Cringle," Tim cracks back in his playful, ringing voice.

The uneasy feeling in the rolling pit of my stomach makes my belly feel chill as ice. And I think of my old mess-mate, Johnny, who died so suddenly last year. Well I recall his fading face and dying eyes piercing into mine, as if I had some personal responsibility for his wounds, which I did not.

And then there are many voices shouting at once—men from amidships, men from the rigging, men by the anchor chain. A seaman on the yardarm shouts, "Shark!"

Tim, twisting fore and aft, yells, "That's a joke."

Tailtackle, at my elbow, remarks, "They done that afore with the lad, teased him 'bout shark this and shark that, so as to throw 'im off balance on the cable as he was a-goin' in."

My eyes are glued on Tim—no shark anywhere in sight, but still the odd, queasy, upsy-daisy feeling in my belly.

Then, out of the dappled depths, there is a monster fish. His dorsal fin breaks surface with a dismal, audible hiss.

"It's just a dolphin," Tailtackle cackles out. But even I know the rushing sound of that predatory fin and what it means, and where it is going in that fury of predatory speed.

"What's all the hollering about, Tom?" Captain Smythe questions, striding up with Peter and Mr. Yerk at his sleeve. "It isn't Tim, is it?"

"Afraid so, sir."

In my ears is a small, thin, pitiless ringing. In my gut, a roly-poly ball of undigested hardtack wishing to come up.

I crack the spell of inaction, however, and run for the gaff hook that is tucked up by the scuppers. Dashing to the cable—I begin to slide down, one hand on the chain, the other on the hook. Out of the corner of my eye, the great fish circles, swings in.

I'm halfway down, and Peter shouts, "Hook a leg."

I do.

The cable begins to shake as tension takes hold of it. Tim is climbing, hauling himself upward, his body half out of the water. I inch closer, readying my gaff. The shark curves, and its glistening white belly glances in the sun and it comes awfully close, turns smoothly, reroutes, comes round again. The taut cable quakes—this time, it's Tim kicking at the shark's head. I aim the gaff hook.

Then, amid the monkey shrieks of the crew, I sink the hook into the beast's bluish gray hide.

The gaff bends away; the shark takes it under with him.

I slide down close and get hold of Tim's right hand. The gaff pops up, the shark just under it. There is a crunch, and the water bubbles with reddish foam.

My legs are locked tightly round the cable.

My left hand's holding Tim's right.

"I've got you, Tim," I tell him, but the gaff's awhirl in the water, and the shark makes a sideways pass, and there is another terrible crunch noise with the water bubbling red; and Tim drops down, his eyes fixed on my face, his hand slipping damply, weakly.

I grab him up just as that gleaming, grinding head jerks him down again with a tremulous, seesawing pulling. Tim's legs below the knee are lost in the boiling redness as the monster shark stirs the channel like punch, his dorsal dancing and the popping gaff going up and down and side to side, and I hold Tim hard, crushing his hand in mine, and his palm's slipping, slipping into the sickening purplish tide.

Then he just seems to melt out of my grasp as in a nightmare and he sinks into that death froth with the shark jerking him, at all possible angles, so that half of his body remains upright like a marionette puppet, stiff and straight, while the other half is gone in the blood-water tide.

Again and again, Tim is borne up and down as the shark controls him completely—and he is neither dead nor alive, but a thing, just a thing that was once human but is now nothing, and I watch helplessly as Tim's gray face wobbles away like a mask, his eyes, frozen from shock, locked on mine, and his lips, yes, his lips mumbling something.

Then—*swifft*—he vanishes.

In a twinkling, all is still.

No one man speaks. The ship is quiet. The hissing fin of the shark shows once more, but no Tim, and with that goes my last hope of ever doing anything good for anyone, ever again; and I dare not look at the faces of the crew, for they are all on me. I can feel their eyes boring into me and their cold, hard, knifelike stares as I come up the cable.

Hard stares, too, as I walk tween-decks to bury my face in my hammock. And cry. Cry like a baby, as they say. Even sob. It isn't manly, but then I'm not a man yet. I'm still a boy in a man's uniform. My eyes are filled with tears that take me back to Johnny's corpse-face . . . now Tim's . . . their identical gold curls pasted to their foreheads . . . their eyes locked on mine, neither accusing nor forgiving but staring into my face. I feel something bump my hammock from underneath—Sneezer's head. He bumps me like this whenever he's worried about me.

He bumps the hammock again—this time hard—and nearly knocks me to the floor.

I climb out and bury my face in his neck fur, still sobbing, and him backing up and licking the salt tears from my eyes, and me remembering a song of Peter Mangrove's—

*Ash to ash,*
*Salt to salt,*
*Me sailor's life,*
*Me own damn fault.*

*At anchor, that evening in the captain's cabin*

I'm sitting on a bench at Captain Smythe's map table, scribbling by lantern light. My own sleeping quarters are immediately next door in the gun room with the other officers, but I cannot write in my log there with everyone's eyes on me.

I suppose you'd say I'm foolish for taking up my pen when I might have a word or two with someone, a civil conversation, as it were. Yet, with whom? My dear friend Peter is on duty, and he and I have already talked about Tim and my failure to rescue him, and why I shouldn't be holding myself to blame.

"A mon 'ave him own life, Tom," he says consolingly. "An' him 'ave him own death, an' him own 'eaven an' hell. We cyaan mek life an' we cyaan stop death. It is just so, you must know."

I nod. Looking into his eyes—so fearless and true—I feel, for the moment, unafraid; maybe even brave. But just for a moment. When it passes, I tremble again, as with the ague, and I even feel that the *vomito* is back again and I am going to die myself.

Captain Smythe, now, is privy to nothing of this and he has said no word to me about my failure. He acts a trifle odd, but I know it is the Madeira wine. The flask is his best friend now, and he acts as if, more than ever, he wants to be left alone.

In any event, he's sleeping as my pen is scratching; and, oh, with what heavy heart do I script these anxious, lonely, late-night thoughts. . . .

"What is it you're scribbling now, Tom?" Captain Smythe asks from his hammock. I jump a foot from my stool when he says this, because I thought the man was asleep and that I was all alone.

"A tallying of bad news, sir," I tell him abruptly.

He sighs louder than the wind at our aft window. "You mean a tolling, don't you?"

"Yes, as of church bells, sir."

He sighs again. The mosquito netting all about his hammock puffs. "All we need now is an albatross," he groans. "Put that in, if you like."

I gather his meaning: An albatross is an eyeful no sailor wishes to see. An omen of such ill portent that it bears nothing if not a sea wreck on its outspread wings.

"Well, put it all in your log. If this voyage holds true to course—or curse—we'll have ample time to know if *owl* is *albatross* spelled with different letters. Heavens if I know, Tom. But you mustn't pummel yourself too much on Tim's account. You did what you could. Your arm wasn't long enough, is all."

I wish he hadn't said that. My shortish arms and littleness are all about the ship. My new nickname is Tom Bungle, or, as some say, Tom Cricket, which they're all saying since the shark attack. Well, it's not just that—it's my being so deuced small. But must I hear it every step I take? I would throw my epaulet overboard and commence my life anew as a cabin boy—if only I could.

Sometimes I long to be done with this horrible life at sea! I promised never to let my father down, but perforce, I must . . . or else more will die at my incompetent boyish hand.

Who wants to be a hero, anyway?

As if hearing my thoughts, Captain Smythe says into the scrivening darkness (I have but a candle burning), "It wasn't you, dear boy. Don't trouble yourself about that. If anyone, it was Halsey and his damnable goat guts. But don't trouble yourself about that, either. It's all trifle wearying, isn't it?"

"Wearying, sir?"

"Life."

"I suppose so, sir."

"You don't know, you're too young. You've lost a few, sure. I've lost hundreds. Have you any idea what *that* means, young scamp?"

Then he shuts up, still as a church on Monday, and says no more, and I am alone, I think, with the cable sounds, the moanings and groanings of the *Kraaken,* which at this late hour seem so alive.

Then, as if sleep-talking, Captain Smythe says hoarsely, "When you hear the seventh bell, lad, relieve Mr. Yerk on deck."

"Yes, sir."

"And, Tom, do something for me, will you?"

"Certainly, sir."

"Check for that villainous shark."

"And what should I do if I see him, sir?"

"Tell Nedrick to dispatch him. I shall sleep fitfully thinking of Tim and the deuced way he stared at *me*—so blank of face."

"He stared at you, sir?"

"Yessss." His voice buzzes off thickly, and a moment later, over the creak and pitch of the ship, Captain Smythe is snoring.

So, I think, amazed . . . he thinks Tim stared at *him*.

*It is our guilty conscience, then. Our each and own, individual, guilty, black-sheep conscience!*

Sleep is one thing, I warrant, that I will not indulge in this night. For, no matter what I write in my log, I hear in my head the dread crunch of bone. As I write, the moths mill about the gold, slender candle flame, and the tree frogs' tinkle in the rock cairns of the cove chinkle brightly and loudly, and the tide ebbs and flows, but sleep, precious sleep, is out of the question.

*After seven bells*

But I think of the dead more than the living. Johnny, who was killed in action aboard the *Bream;* Obed, who was drowned in the dark waters off this selfsame Cuban coast—his broad smile and laughing eyes follow me everywhere I go. I should think of my father who died, but I do not; I perversely think of Obed and the night he sat on the windowsill of Cinnamon Hill Great House—not *him* but his *ghost*—the night that I was so trembly from the Fever.

Whether he was a dream or a phantom I may never know, but he did come back from the dead to put into my palm his one worldly treasure, a jewel-studded dagger, and whether or not one believes in ghosts, duppies, ghoulies, or phantoms, the dagger was real (it is safe in my mother's keeping), and now you know why I can't stop thinking about Obed, for after he showed himself to me that way, I began to think that the dead really do come back from the grave!

But whether they are mad at us, for what we did or didn't do, in life, I do not know . . . or, I should say, I fear to know. . . .

*Sometime after, midwatch*

I am out on deck with Sneezer. Midnight clear. Nice night, no fog. Staring into the quiet channel, the first bell rings, telling me that it is already 12:30. The half hour gone and me not knowing where it went—suddenly I see a phosphorescence skimming along the water's surface, not one chain (sixty feet) from where I stand by the fo'c'sle. Sneezer sees it, too. His claws clatter; he jumps to the rail.

Twelve feet long, this must be the very shark that murdered

Tim. With a flick of the tail, the giant fish disappears. I stare into the dark and discern his pointed head. His toothsome jaw, his huge, fluid, fleshy body.

Shimmery wake of sparkles streams astern of him. For a moment he is at rest, suspended motionless in the gin-clear, moonlit canal, aglide, slowly, faintly moving.

Mr. Yerk, who, when I relieved him, was set to go belowdecks, remains with me now to have a pipe smoke. He touches my elbow, his narrow, bone-clean face quite close to mine. He sucks at the stem of his pipe and squirts a jet of smoke into the moist air. "Been watching the loikes of 'im all night, sir," he says.

"Go get Nedrick now," I order. "And see to it he has his sharpshooter's eye well opened and his best gun well primed."

Mr. Yerk departs in haste, the fragrant smoke following him like a ghostly wake.

I glance down at the water where the beast was last seen, but the thing has gone without a trace. The canyon walls, overhung with creepers like the towers of the hanging gardens of Babylon, are steep and dank, and chinking with those noisy singing frogs.

Leaning along the rail, I hear the scuffling of bare feet—then, there's Nedrick with his odd caterpillar eyebrows and his curly copper hair. "Look, carefully into the stream," I tell him.

He does so, peering sharply. If there is a man who sees better than anyone, including yours truly, it is Mr. Nedrick. He can put out a gnat's eye at sixty steps.

Together, in insufferable silence, we watch the clear water, and then there is a curious sparkling—a curving, carving tail.

Nedrick whispers, "Why, it's the veery mownster as murthered poor little Tim this veery mornin', yeer honor." He speaks low and soft in his huskiest Scottish brogue, which, I must confess, I have a real liking for.

Then he puts in, "I know 'im from the gash you gave 'im under his larboard blinker . . . you done it, good and clean, with your boat hook."

A rush of warmth runs to my cheeks.

I hadn't realized I had punished the brute—in the horror of losing Tim, I forgot how I buried my gaff under his eye. Now, even in darkness, we can see the hook whistling crisply through the limpid channel.

"A veritable water *kelpie*," he mutters, raising his rifle to take aim. "'Twill make a turrible racket, sir, when I squeeze off." Then, eyeing me, he continues his soft slurring. "You does want me to put out his blinkers, doesn't you, sir?"

The *sir*s and *honor*s seem to restore some of my lost self-respect.

"That I does, er, do, Nedrick."

"To even the score, suchlike." He gives me a cruel and kindly wink.

"Mr. Nedrick—before you shoot—what do you mean by a water kelpie?"

"You know, a *merperson*—half seal and half human, but capable of turrible woes, sahr!"

"I prefer to think of him as a shark," I tell him.

"Not for long," he adds, winking weirdly, and sighting.

All this passes in seconds, and I watch as he lifts the long gun level with the rail and snuggles his face into position, as if almost kissing the oaken stock, and then settling the barrel, iron to iron, and softly stroking the trigger, he clicks back the hammer.

Then, snug as Christmas, he points the long gun into the last phosphorescence. For a time the sounds of the tinkling frogs are all we hear, along with the sometime creaking of the rigging and the *Kraaken* slumbering and sighing, and then a school of sea trout gleam, suddenly, glance quickly, skip upon the surface, and then the gaffed shark is back, turning wheels round the cable line, hopeful of more meat, perhaps, and the top fin behind it, and Mr. Nedrick exhales once, quite noisily. "The damnable baste," he says—then a flash of light, a spurt of flame, a blast of holy thunder—and, *clap,* the killer rolls on its back, spirals all about, and the rimrocks bang with echoes near and far, and the ship comes awake as a hundred men snap up in their hammocks.

"Are you going to fire again, Mr. Nedrick?"

"Yeer honor, sir," says he, "I think ye'll find it unness-a-saree, sahr."

"Indeed?"

The violent thrashing continues, as does the aftershot. But now there are many men on deck—a lot of crew with the sleep still sewn into their eyelids and their mouths agape. All are staring witless now at the great shark rolling in its throes.

Particles of silver—the stirred phosphorescence in a whirlpool of whiteness—fanning out in a circle, and the whole thing is such a spectacle of revenge, I feel my heart thudding out of control! Strange, somehow, that Captain Smythe hears it not. Anyway, he doesn't appear beside me, which is so odd, as he was the one who wanted the creature dead.

Mr. Yerk is there, close by, and Peter Mangrove, admiring the two of us. I can see that everyone's well pleased that the animal responsible for Tim's death has been duly caught and punished.

I thrill to their applause. And, as quickly as they loathed me, they seem now to like me. But soon the shark sinks below our sight, going down until nothing can be seen of it but a tiny point of silver.

And I whisper to Peter, "Am I vindicated, then?"

He quickly nods, his eyes warming to the magic of the night. "Yuh even de score, Tom," he says, and he places a warm hand on my shoulder, and Sneezer jumps up and puts his huge paws on my shoulders.

*June 9, 1813*
*The following morning . . .*

About an hour and a half before day-dawn, I am up from a strange dream of my old, dead nemesis, Jenkins. In the dream he is beating Sneezer on the head with a brass-buckled Navy shoe. I run to protect my dog and, confronting Jenkins, I see his face all disfigured, melted like candle wax from the brow down. He looks, all smooth and hairless, like the shark that killed Tim, and I awaken gasping, choking on my own spit.

It is the boatswain at my side. "Sir," he says, chuckling. "Are you in the teeth of something?"

"What do you want?"

"All hands up anchor," he says. Then the gun room steward comes up with his too-bright lantern, and I blink uncertainly, and he sternly reminds us, "Gentlemen, all hands . . ."

I am up and out in the beat of a heart, up on deck, with the fever-dream still caught in my craw.

***Sometime after . . .***

Now, lest you ever imagine that, because I am an officer, my privacy is secure, my station elevated on the *Kraaken,* let me hasten to say that the captain's cabin occupies the after part of the ship. Next to it, on the same deck, is the gun room. In a corvette such as the *Kraaken,* the gun room's twenty feet long by twelve wide. Lighted by a long scuttle, or skylight, in the deck above.

Now, on each side of the gun room runs a little row of chambers, just for officers, complete with chest of drawers, basin stand, and wooden-framed hammock that is six feet long and two feet wide. Each room has a private door and window—

a far cry from what I had last year, I can tell you.

The sleeping hammock is slung from cleats nailed to the beams above, while lanyards fastened by rings suspend it in the air. What holds us in is a small strip of canvas running from head to foot on each side.

The center of the gun room's got a long table flanked by a wooden bench with a high back to it. The large, clumsy chair at the head of the table is for Captain Smythe, while I sit at the other end. A sideboard behind the table's well stocked with knives, forks, spoons, tumblers, and cups, all of which are made fast to the deck by cleats and staples and bands of spun yarn so as to prevent them fetching away in a pitch of the sea. There, now, you have the whole of it.

### *Weighing anchor*

So, I am up on deck and at station. The gun's fired by Mr. Nedrick, and we weigh anchor. I'm so relieved to be getting free of this horrible place, I can barely write without making my words look like so much spilled ink. . . .

Cables are on either side of the *Kraaken* and these are being drawn portside by a string of Santiago mules. In no time, we are back out of that unsafe little harbor. Then, turning about, we run out upon the tide to seek the deeper, safer blue beyond the toothy reef.

Fortunately, our going out is swifter than our coming in, and we scrape but once along the reef rocks. Then we're running at about four knots, with the land wind right after us.

Once we are clear of the channel, the sea breeze finally catches us. We make sail, to southward and eastward, under close-reefed topsail, jib, and spanker.

"All right, then, pipe to breakfast," Captain Smythe cracks to Mr. Yerk.

"Sail abeam of us to windward," I add, for I see something untoward in my glass on the horizon.

"What is she, Mr. Cringle? You know I can't see past my nose."

"Brig, sir."

"Pennant?"

"None I can make out."

"How's she steering?"

"Edging away, sir."

"Let's go to breakfast anyway. Mr. Yerk, crack on. We'll overhaul the swaggerer soon enough. Tom, come with me, we've got to eat before we fight."

All eager for food, Captain Smythe chuckles at my ear. "Well, Tom? You think it's the *Hornet* again?"

"I believe so, sir."

"Go to breakfast anyhow," he says.

I wonder—is he at it again? But I see no winking flask . . . he seems sober enough.

"Tell the men to go below; put a man at helm, quartermaster and signalman at the ready. Understood, Mr. Yerk?"

Mr. Yerk nods smartly to the captain. "Seen, sir."

Yerk bobs his head and ducks round to see the signalman's position in the fore-rigging.

"Sir," I say, "we cannot go eat when danger's looming." Then, soft and inconspicuous, I whisper near his ear, "The *albatross,* remember, sir?"

"Well, Tom—coming?" he says, not hearing. He gives me a bleary, muttonchopped grin.

"I've a funny feeling, sir. I ought to stay on deck."

"Are you *questioning* me, Mr. Cringle?"

Mr. Yerk barks, "Captain, Cringle's right, she's turning round."

The signalman in the fore-rigging calls down, "She's flashing signal, sir. Seems she's got something for us."

"Very well, then," Captain Smythe moans. "Let the men have their bloody breakfast . . . I'll forgo mine. Tack, Mr. Yerk, tack. Stand toward her."

I turn round and give her a going-over with the glass. My stomach rolls. Not only am I terribly hungry, but now, suddenly sick with anxiousness. As the brig billows on, Captain Smythe orders, "Shorten sail, Mr. Yerk." There is reason for my unease: The sea is clear, the water is fine, the clouds puffed up like potato mash. When things look bright, the dark lining is soon to show.

Moreover, this brig looks exactly like the one we were chasing. A slaver full of Maroons, those blacks who steal away from plantations only *to be stolen* themselves and thence to be sold off in such cities as New Orleans, Charleston, Savannah, and Manhattan.

I may wonder at Captain Smythe's offhand manner about this . . . but the fact is, rum and port do more than trick the eye; very likely they swab the mind of reason. Well, he is less himself than he used to be, but what he is now I do not fully know.

Presently the boatswain's whistle rings, and the gravelly

voice of Mr. Catwell, the cannoneer and whistle-blower, grates throughout the ship. The men come in a trice, tumbling over one another to get to their tasks—shortening sail . . . foresail and mainsail go up as the jib comes down . . . in topgallant sails . . . back the main-topsail.

By heaving to, in this way—turning around—we bring the big, dark ship on our weather bow. She is now within a cable's length of us.

Captain Smythe, pigtail to the wind, stands on the second foremost gun, larboard side. Oddly enough, he is showing some interest. There is nothing like a skirmish to get the blood going, I guess, but I confess, for the most part, the man seems to have lost everything but that damnable appetite for food and wine.

Then—all of a sudden—he's back to where he was when I first met him. A starchy senior officer with a whiplash tongue.

"Mr. Cringle," he commands, "get me my trumpet."

I run to the cabin and fetch it for him. As I hand it up, he asks, "What's the name of the ship . . . I cannot for the likes of me see it . . . my poor eyes! Oh, well, this is more exciting than breakfast, is it not, Mr. Cringle?"

"She calls herself the *Hornet,*" I say.

"Take another look, man."

I scan the *Hornet*'s deserted deck with my glass—not a soul to be seen.

"What see you there, Mr. Cringle?"

"They've hauled in their topgallant sails. She'll soon bear up against us. But, sir, I see no men."

"Not one?"

"None, sir."

Through the glass, I study her masts, dark to windward. There's little else to see . . . except for a few chickens roosting in the rigging.

I tell Captain as much and watch his eyebrows rise.

Smacking his lips, he spits off the gun perch into the sea. "The deuce!" he rages, swinging his head about. His pigtail, anchored down with a little marlinespike, swings in an arc in back of his head.

"I don't like repeat performances, Tom," he mutters to me. Then to Mr. Yerk, he says, "Put the helm up—keep her away a bit—steady—that'll do."

Captain Smythe's fat, red face bores into mine. "I'm going to slap a shot across her bows, Tom."

"Well, considering our past experience, sir . . . but, still, I don't know."

"I hope you said chickens and not albatrosses."

I manage a small smile, but the empty deck and the spooky ship give me no conversational ease: I still remember the jar she gave us. A heavy feeling of dread has gotten deep into my core like a worm in the old apple.

"All right, Mr. Cringle, tell Mr. Catwell to prime the long gun."

I have a very bad feeling about firing on this unknown vessel. "Shall we send a private signal first, sir?" I ask.

He gives me a mean, squinched stare.

"I mean, sir, just in case she's got sickness onboard—or something else."

"Very well, Mr. Cringle, for the sake of sickness I shall give the order for a private signal, but let's stand by the long gun. I don't like this ship one little bit—open the magazine, will you?"

I pass the order on to Mr. Catwell, who calls for the signal up top, and it is carried out. But the signal flashes on dead eyes or hidden ones, and the notion of a ruse deepens in my own mind—and Captain's, too, I think.

Mr. Catwell, in shabby shirt and felt shoes and with gunpowder smeared all across his brow, looks to me for another order. He is a large man, who moves with the quickness and softness of a fat, contented cat, which is appropriate, considering his name.

"This brig's the devil, Mr. Cringle," says Captain Smythe. "Won't speak or heave to."

"Sir?"

"Yes, Mr. Cringle."

"You've not notified them with your trumpet, sir. It's common practice . . . under the circumstances."

"All right," he replies. Putting his mouthpiece to his lips, he calls out, "Be seen, or we shall send a round shot between your masts! Do you hear? Respond, at once!"

The big, corky ship bobs innocently in the sea trough, but she makes no sign of having heard, except far up in the rigging, a rooster lets loose a raucous *cock-a-doodle-doo* and causes all the men to laugh . . . nervously, I think.

"Ready, sir?" presses Mr. Catwell, torch in hand.

"Fire," says Captain Smythe.

Mr. Catwell's cannon sends off a shot that wracks the brig's deck with a *whunk*—then we hear a melancholy howl . . . and nothing else.

Some of the men start to laugh, but Captain Smythe silences them with a wave of the hand.

"Was that Sneezer?" asks bald Mr. Yerk, rubbing his open palm across his round, clean skull. I wonder how he could miss the big dog at my side, but his eyes are peeled elsewhere. Just then, in answer to the wail, Sneezer emits a funny little whine of his own.

It comes again—the most ungainly noise you ever heard. From deep tween-decks, in the emboweled timbers of the brig's bow. Again, Sneezer responds with a mournful howl of his own.

"The deuce's daughter!" cries Mr. Catwell, shaking his flaxen head and tugging at his corn silk chin-whiskers.

In the chop of waves, the foreshortened sails of the mystery brig clap out—*pop, pop*—and the sea trough between us gives a shove, and we heave up as the brig goes down, and then we hear that ghostly cry—a cross between a howl and a scream—nothing human ever made such a sound, I can tell you that!

"By Jove, if I didn't know better, I'd say it came from the throat of a dog! In fact, *your dog,* Mr. Cringle." Captain Smythe looks me bluely in the eye and sends a jet spittle through the split in his front teeth off the side of his cannon perch.

"Sneezer's not so baleful as all that, sir."

He grins. "Of course he isn't, lad." Then he roughs Sneezer's head with his open palm.

"What if it's a bunch of sick sailors, sahr?" Mr. Nedrick questions from the larboard.

Captain Smythe, his face drawn up like a purse, answers, "I won't be called a murderer if there's any sailors dying onboard! Tom, pick some worthy lads—you're going to have to board her."

A moment later, the grapplings are in place—one round the backstay, the other through the chain plate. So the two ships are joined, helm to helm.

"We're set to board, sir."

"All right, Tom, shake a leg, will you?"

I take hold of the boarding hemp with Peter Mangrove, Mr. Tailtackle (believe it or not, he is one deuce of a hand-to-hand fighter), plus steady Mr. Nedrick and all of his sharpies.

Peter has girded himself with his sash and stuck his pistol and his dirk into it. Good, brave Peter. Always there when I need him, and often when I don't. Just the sight of his sea-hardened face, all whittled with resolve, is enough to inspire even a fainthearted fellow. He may have a wooden leg—carved, they say, from the spar of Admiral Nelson's ship—but he is better balanced on it than any two-legger I know.

"You and Peter start off; the rest'll follow."

"She standing down for us, Tom," Peter remarks, nodding at the brig. We are seesawing; she is down and we are up, but right now, we're evenstephen, so I take the boarding rope hanging from a larboard fore-yardarm and push off from the safe rail of the *Kraaken.*

We're so near, I might have jumped the distance, but with arms and all, we are better off doing it this way. Red-whiskered Nedrick poises back a ways in the netting, waiting. On deck the rest of the mariners are at quarters at the guns, tubs of wadding and boxes of grape all ready and ranged, for the signal to fire.

So this is it! We are on a three-hundred-ton, seemingly abandoned brig, the *Hornet.* A vessel with full sides round as a pumpkin. Scrubbed clean as slate, and yet—fo'c'sle and poop, foredeck and aft—are dead, empty of life. . . .

"I've the worst bloody feeling about this, Peter," say I.

He has his nose to the breeze, as if scenting something. "Dis ship fully loaded, Tom."

I don't know whether he's talking about the ten ports and nine guns of a side, or the hold being full of men, munitions, and booty—and before I can ask him, there's a horrible, queer noise belowdecks—neither man nor animal but something of the two combined—and it sounds full of malice . . . but what the deuce it is, there isn't time to guess!

I touch my heavy leather belt, finger my primed pistol and my sharpened sword, and we proceed, unhindered, to the main forward hatch, grim faced but determined. And then we begin the descent into darkness, oblivion, and the awfulest smell I've ever smelled . . . something like tar and excrement and sloshy, stinky bilge.

### *Belowdecks on the Hornet*

Quite distinctly, I hear the sound of labored breathing. All is dark, and whoever, or whatever, has a bellows for lungs and a right tuneful way of sucking air, from the sound of things.

For a moment, I stand on the last rung in the black, bleaky hold. How dark is it? Like pitch, it is—the only light being the open fore-scuttle hatch, which admits the sun and makes a fat, buttery square at the foot of the ladder. Standing there, not yet ready to release the ladder's link to the upper world, I hang by one hand and one foot, sort of suspended, waiting. I can feel my heart bumping against my ribs.

That nasty smell . . . what *is* it?

A noise comes out of the stinky, inky darkness . . . a grumbling, a gargling, and a gnashing all at the same time.

Then the heavy, coarse, in-and-out sucking of air . . . of a monster! What else would make such a hellish, awful sound?

I look at Peter, just above on the fore-scuttle landing. Cutlass drawn, he awaits my command.

I look back into the shroudy black . . . what if it's just some chuckleheaded swab who's had too much schnapps and is sleeping it off on the broad lid of a sea chest?

Peter is itching to be down with me. He whispers, "What a-gwan dere, Tom?"

Looking level with the night hold and breathing in that

godforsaken stink, I call out—there being nothing better to do—"Halloo!"

No answer.

A snoring grunt, punctuated by more noisome breathings, pulsings, and drunken gulpings of air.

Peter whispers, "Some fool walkin' off de land o' dreams."

"Let's wake him up, then."

Up high, abovedecks, I hear the loose canvas of the jib, snapping and quailing, slapping in the breeze. I wish I had a lantern right about now—but I don't.

Peter sighs, in his halo of sunlight, "Sometin' 'bout dis me don' love, Tom! Me tell yuh true."

The breathing symphony raises in volume.

I can almost feel the heat of it on my face.

"If you be alive, wake up, mon, an' answer to the king's Royal Navy!" This is Peter's best and most official summons, but what comes back is the low, insistent, and insolent sound of a drunken man about to beat someone with a club. A kind of *r-r-r-r-r-r-ing,* going up in scale and rising, too, in urgent, angry inflection of someone all set to charge.

Down along the grim forecastle go I—poor, brave, foolhardy Tom Cringle, and at each little move I make, I say a little, small, pitiful prayer in the face of this spine-tingling soon-to-come assault. This whole time I sense that, at any moment, I'll be smashed to smithereens. But I have my pistol posted, and my other hand is on the handle of my sword, when, turning round smartly in a circle, I feel something hot as Hades blowing straight into my face—and then I am off the floor, footloose and fancy-free, swirling every which way, flailing like a man made of straw, and it is all done in the most awful, the most blindful, blackety-black hold, which smells of fish heads and bitter-sour urine, and things worse than that, too.

My pistol's dislodged from my right hand and falls with a *blang* to the hard board of the deck. My groping left hand seizes a handful of my huge foe's oafish garment—and what a shaggy, baggy coat he has on, a pea jacket of immense proportions.

What a monstrous sailor, what a Gargantua, and his breath—good God, it is as from the fetid interior of a rotten carcass.

"Help!" I choke. "He's got me!"

Whereupon Peter lands, foot first—then comes his peg banging down like Neptune's staff—he's beside us. I feel the body of the thing standing firm, so I pull at his fur-collared pea jacket, and he growls at me all the while. Then his hairy-knuckled hand smashes into my face and knocks me out. I hear chains chinking and clanking and all other kinds of diabolical, devilish, whimsy sounds. Whoever this is, he's a prisoner and wants his freedom worse than I want mine—or in equal proportion. But now I'm afloat on a sea of dreams, only half-awake and aware that Peter's carrying on the fight without me, as I am being hugged and hauled all round in a dizzying dance like the proverbial gallows jigger.

Then I am flung free and clear. The hateful prisoner's gruff response to Peter's severe counterattack from behind.

Madly, I scramble to get away, scuttling crablike across the deck—but he, the big man, jerks me to my feet—alas, he has me again.

I shimmy out of his grasp for the second time, and, once

more, the mad seaman lunges at me, growling his fury and ringing his chains, and I yell out, "Peter, I'm waylaid!"

After that, I'm hugged up in another of those clutches. The man's embracing me with his arms, as if resolved we shall never part; and, oh, his breath's so hot and rotten and I am just dangling as if a lifeless puppet, and my face is sort of joined cheek to chest against his scratchy body hair.

So, while this galoof's squeezing the wind out of me and doing a shambly dance across the deck with his chains ringing, Peter is thwacking him on the back with his pistol handle—but all to no avail.

"Mercy! Murder! Blood! Fire!" I yell—my voice growing feeble as I run out of air and I start to see stars, and the darkness grows darker still.

I make a last effort to free my right hand. At the same time, Peter pounds the blackguard's head with his pistol—and then, lights out, I know what a hanged man feels like when the floor drops out beneath his feet and he tiptoes on the sky.

Then there is no more light. My eyelids flutter.

My knees buckle. I am about to pass out.

Then I get a gulp of air and I slip out from under him. He gropes for me in the dark. Peter delivers a bone-cracking strike to the man's skull. Finally, the brute goes down into his pile of chains.

Weakly, I scramble away. And fumble into a heavy cargo net. I get to my knees and, gathering the net in my arms, stand up and throw this thing over the insane drunk giant, who has almost crushed the life out of me.

Then Peter and I head up the fore-scuttle, where, safe on top, we stare down and see our opponent clearly and well for the first time. There he sits in his little pool of sun, all draped out in cargo net, his head bowed, his feet splayed—and now I know why I couldn't budge him and also why he almost crushed me like a worm: The drunken giant with the hairy chest is not human. He is a great brown bear, now growling and, for the moment, so balled up in net, he's no worry to anyone.

*That evening, aboard the Kraaken*

"Well done, Tom." Captain Smythe grins as Surgeon Jigmaree patches my scratches, and Peter's, too, in the captain's cabin.

"I scarce know what good we did, sir."

"You're both heroes," says Captain Smythe.

"Who get cut up like a salt cod in the paws of a chained bear."

Captain Smythe smiles and the space between his piano-key front teeth widens like a portal.

"Well, Tom, no time for modesty. You fought and bested a bear—you and Peter—and, believe me, that animal was placed just so, and that ship abandoned just so, all to an unfathomable purpose . . . yet, I must confess to knowing what it is."

"Ouch!" I cry as Jigmaree, the only man my height on the whole ship, splashes virgin bay rum on the ravine over my right eye.

"To *what* purpose, then?" I ask, wincing.

Captain Smythe, pacing the floor, hands clasped behind his back, stops, whirls sharp at heel. He wears trousers and boots, and his open shirt, unpleasantly enough, reveals his double-girth of stomach.

The captain's cabin is stifling, but it smells a good deal fresher than that bear's lair, be assured of that.

"Well, that'll be all, Mr. Cringle. You'll heal soon enough in the salt air." Sneezer wags his tail in approval and gives me a dollop of face-licking that hurts a good deal more than I let on.

Mr. Jigmaree clicks shut his leather bag and exits promptly. He has cleaned Peter, stem to stern, but then he has fewer abrasions than me, being my backup man. Now he sits opposite me at table, shaking his head, murmuring, "Me sooner face a duppy den a *bear!*"

Captain Smythe, still pacing, soberly, mulls over my question. "Their purpose, as I see it, was to draw off our attention, so as to slip away—and that the scoundrels did exceeding well."

"You think there were two ships, sir?"

"Indeed I do, Tom."

Captain Smythe comes over to where I am sitting on my stool, bare chested and smelling sweetly of bay leaves. "You see, Tom, while you and Peter brawled with their bear, they sailed off neatly without anyone's noticing. A clever ploy!"

"How could that be?" I ask, touching my tender wounds here and there with my index finger.

"As easy as netting the bear," he guffaws.

Peter frowns, as do I. "Dat were no way *easy* ting, sir," he laments.

"No, sir, it was *not,*" I confirm. "By the way, what do we do with the animal?"

"We can send a transport back for him; a creature like that is worth plenty for show."

"And what of the guard ship?"

Captain Smythe scowls. "They will be back to pick up their cargo."

"Wha—you—mean—dat nasty old bear?" queries Peter.

Captain Smythe grimaces. "Not the bear, confound it, but whatever's clanking chains down there."

"That was the bear," say I, forcefully.

"I'll be mummified if it's not something else," Captain Smythe avows. "What I've been saying all along."

"It smelled rank and thick down there," I remark. "But I thought it was just the beast."

"I'll wager that the ship's full of stolen slaves, taken right off the island of Jamaica."

After dressing, I am ordered to go with Peter and scan the horizon; and sure enough, just as Captain Smythe said, there now claps a clean, white sail close aboard of us, and to windward. Old Captain, muddled though he is *most* of the time, is, *some* of the time, sharp as a cooper's tack.

*June 10, 1813*
*Shortly after daybreak on the morrow*

That sunlit sail keeps astern of us—but I cannot make out more than that; neither her true size, nor her veritable rig from this far-off hazy distance. So here we are waiting and passing the glass (not grog, of course, but rather the spyglass) while Mr. Catwell and Mr. Nedrick and some others go tween ships.

With torches and arms, they descend into that hold of maelstrom, and salvage—exactly as Captain Smythe prophesied—ten slaves, iron linked, heads bowed, and squatting miserably in their own filth.

So, as we, Captain Smythe and myself, hold watch, the hammers chink, and soon these poor, bedraggled prisoners, rawboned and bleeding from open sores, are relinquished of their fetters. Captain Smythe, shaking his head, says to me, "You know, Tom, there's no law that forbids slavery, as such, wretched though it be. There is only a sketchy maritime act to prevent transport of slaves."

I have my eyes on the leaden horizon and the luffing sail when I ask, "How do we punish the slavers, sir?"

With both hands gripping the rail, and leaning forward, he replies, "We'll have that brig coming up on us for armed encounter, you can be certain."

"Sir, you're that sure they'll fire on us?"

"Or we on them, I cannot yet tell which it will be. But there is another question, too, and that is, what in tarnation will we do with these fellows?"

We look on as they cross the transom. They are all African Coramantees, staring at us with eyes unused to sunshine. I pity them—no, I feel *for* them—as if their sufferation were my own, and, truth be known, it is; it is all of ours, in equal portion.

"If I didn't know better," Captain Smythe remarks, "I'd swear those fellows know you, Tom."

He removes his wig, folds it like a pelt, and puts it into his great coat pocket. "Hotter than a helmet," he tells me, "you should thank the Lord you don't wear one."

The gathered slaves are now aboard the *Kraaken,* their hands and wrists close together, as if they were still bound to one another.

I study their faces as they walk past. For a moment I imagine these are some of the same men I saw at Cranston's Cinnamon Hill plantation while I was recovering there from the ague.

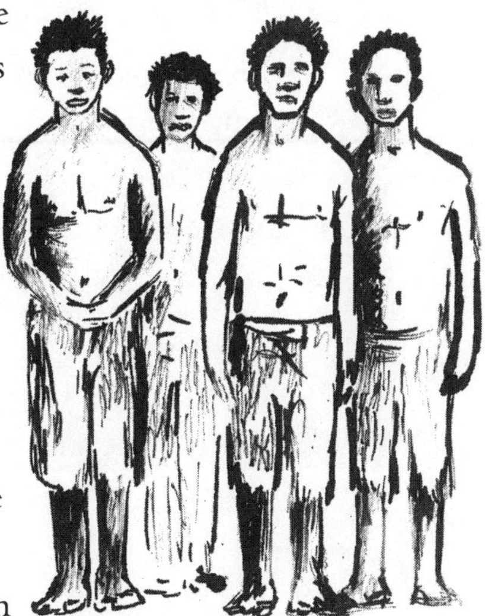

"It's going to be war when that guard ship draws near," Captain Smythe proclaims; then, pausing to spit, he says, "The question is, do we arm these men? Are they to be trusted? We can use every hand we can get."

"If any of these slaves are from Cinnamon Hill, I'd trust them."

Captain Smythe looks dubiously at me. "How so, Tom?"

"Mr. Cranston allowed a great privilege of freedom there. I saw it with my own eyes."

"All right, let's have Peter parlay with them and find out, and if it be so, let them fight with us against our mutual enemy—these brutal American thieves."

"Sir, they are coming hard astern right now."

Peter turns back from the Coramantees and says, "Dem see us at Cinnamon Hill, Tom, so dem mus' be de same men dat work dere all de while."

Captain Smythe nods. "Give these men arms, Mr. Nedrick."

This is done, and the long gun, our heaviest weapon, is slewed round and both carronades are run out and then all three of our artillery are loaded, double shotted, and primed, and all under the worthy supervision of quiet Mr. Catwell.

"Do you see her distinct now, sir?" I ask. Captain Smythe, Mr. Yerk, Peter, and I are all on the fo'c'sle. He faces me and says that he does.

All of us can see our enemy rise, high and dark to windward, like some mighty specter walking the deep.

From our topgallant sail, Mr. Tailtackle calls down, "She's hauling up her courses, taking in sails, bearing up 'cross our bows—mind she don't rake us! She's coming on hard as iron, sir." All this bellowing from above and over the wind, and, all the same, we can see what he is saying as it enacts before our eyes even at this lower level, because she is close now, quite close.

*Within the forward hour*

A chase is on, and I am the one giving orders, rapid-fire. "Stand by the long gun, Mr. Catwell . . . Tailtackle, flash them a warning. . . ." And no sooner are these things done than the spectral guardian ship, all deathly darkness and silence, plows on through the heaves, while Captain Smythe cries, "The deuce!" at my side, jabbing his arms akimbo and standing stiff as a stork.

"Does it always have to be so deucedly dangerous—"

"And mysterious, sir," I finish.

To which he nods and says nothing more on this score. So I command Mr. Yerk to put the helm up. "Keep her away a bit and steady," I say, "and have Mr. Catwell fire a small gun over her bows."

"You're doing right well, lad," Captain Smythe congratulates me, and I feel a sudden pricking under my collar, as if it is too tight to contain myself, which is true—though it is not the tightness, but the pleasure of his compliment that I feel.

Now the strange sail is on our quarter.

Captain Smythe confides in my ear, "I don't like this ship. Have Catwell stand by the long gun."

I tell Mr. Catwell to do so and then I ask Peter to climb aloft and find out what Tailtackle is seeing up there. For some reason the man is no longer talking to us but just staring openmouthed as we shorten sail.

Presently, our adversary counters by getting the foretack onboard again and setting his topgallant sails—all cleverly done because he sees his maneuver, crossing our bows, is foiled by our bearing up so. If you cannot imagine this, try to visualize two armor-laden horses turning at close quarter, flank to flank, and head to head, swiping, missing, aiming forward once again, turning back—but all with precision and great seeming slowness of action so that it all happens in a dreamlike sort of way.

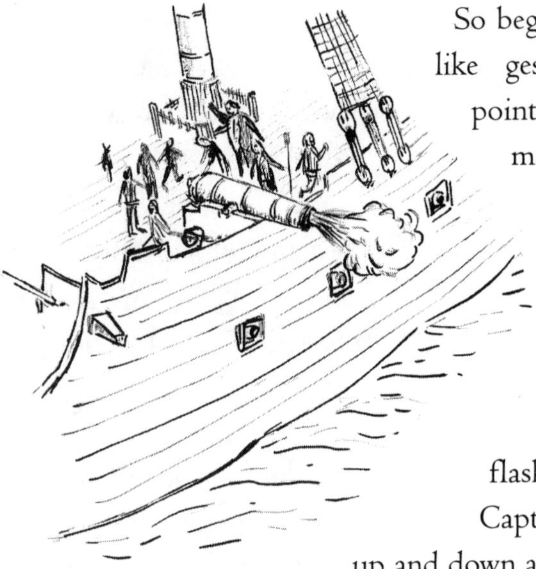

So begins our first really warlike gesture. The long gun points directly between their masts; Captain Smythe cannot help himself, he shouts at Mr. Catwell, "Right between, d'ya hear—are you ready?" And then I see the flask, silver in the sun.

Captain Smythe is hopping up and down and waving the flask and then sucking on it. Mr. Catwell, cool as a cat in a cucumber patch, dances round the side of his great cannon in his funny, felt, soundless shoes, and he barks, "Ready, sir," and Captain Smythe spits between his teeth and hits me on the toe of my boot, and all on deck can hear him holler, "Fire!"

The big gun goes off with a kick and a cloud of smoke, and then the hesitation—and the loudest boom of all—and there is a smashing strike onboard the guard brig, and this is followed by many screams and yells.

"Aye, but the shot has told the tale, sir," Mr. Catwell calls in smartly, licking at his whiskers.

Same time, Peter from aloft: "Dey've shortened sail, Tom!" At which instant, their foresail rises and the enemy lets go his bow gun.

Peter slides down and slips up to my ear. "Nine guns of a side, as I am a sinner," he swears, all out of breath. And again we let drive our long gun and carronade, but the enemy is quick, very quick.

Once more they haul their wind and make sail as close as they can swagger, while firing plentifully at us.

Captain Smythe, Peter, and I duck. A shower of pale splinters sting the sheets—some of these are six inches long; splinters like darning needles—and scatter men everywhere on deck, including our armed contingent of slaves, who, all things considered, are acting as nobly as any fighting crew I've seen under such attack.

Mr. Nedrick, in loud brogue: "Stand by, laddies, take good aim now, and fire!" They do so, too, these black men who moments ago were prisoners. They shoot accurately and well, pelting into the enemy's rigging. I look on, amazed, as a few of our enemy's sharpshooters drop from the sails and thump, lifelessly, on the deck of the brig.

So goes the fray: We're up, and they're down. Or they're up, and we're down. And there is no telling who is winning, if anyone is, or who is losing, if anyone is.

We crowd everything in chase; our enemy has the heels, as they say, and within the hour he is right to windward, so I say, "Keep at him, Mr. Yerk," and I dive tween-decks to consult the chart . . . but there on the surgeon's mess table are three black men splintered deep—arms and legs deeply sliced and pincushioned.

It's a bloody mess, it is, but these brave men are smiling and chewing on biscuits, and thinking little of it . . . tougher men I've never seen in battle. They act as if this thing was all that they lived for. Of course, they were—moments ago—locked in irons. They were going to the Carolinas, and now they are fighting the very ones who captured them.

Mr. Jigmaree, glaring over his nose-perch specs, says to one of the Africans, "Beg pardon, but I must perform an ugly operation on your arm."

I glance that way to see what sterling the fellow's made of and notice that the splinter is driven like a nail into his upper arm. "Doctor, can I be of use?" I ask. "No skill, but steady nerves."

"Can you swathe a bandage, Mr. Cringle?" Mr. Jigmaree asks, peering peckishly over his glasses.

"I've been known to do so."

"Excellent, lad—er, sir," he corrects as he ties a tourniquet to the man's upper arm and clips a surgeon's clamp to the splinter. Then, without warning, he jerks the clamp away, and the injured man smiles as a spigot of blood fountains forth, spattering my shirtfront and my chart.

The wounded fellow's eyes are deep on mine. The splinter, for all this, is a bloodred dagger dripping. But it's out—in Mr. Jigmaree's clamp—and he is forcing the blood spigot, the spurting artery in the man's arm, to quit jetting all over us.

In a few minutes' time, the man is sitting up taking some grog and eating a biscuit—and I wish we had thirty such men in our employ.

"What's your name, man?" say I.

He smiles and answers, "Dem call me Bulla."

"Rest well. We need good men such as yourself."

Back on deck, I see that my worse suspicions are correct: The brig is slipping off. Still in sight, somewhat, but distant—damaged from our blows (as we are from hers) and caroming toward the northeast Jamaican coast, of which, by my reckoning, we are quite near.

***Somewhere off the Jamaican coast, near Falmouth, at sundown***

At watch—scribbling, as usual, between orders.

Here's how it goes:

First we chase—then she chases—then we give her the slip—then she rounds far and away—then we both draw near and pound each other.

Finally, the wind dies away altogether—*outsweeps* is the word we use. I think we've gone ten hours into this little cat-and-mouse chase. Little chance—there being no wind—of subduing her. Frustrating, too, seeing those sails the whole forenoon—large and little, by turns.

She's ahead of us by a league when she catches the luckiest breeze of all, and sprints out of sight. No chance of doubling back and reclaiming her prize, however—that will be ours.

The slave ship *Hornet,* which Captain Smythe had the good sense to anchor down and extra-burden with stone from our hold . . . well, that ship will hang in the breach—or until we "fetch her up back," as Peter says.

Truth to tell, I'm not disheartened at this. I say to Peter, "The brig's surely slipping away." He gives me his cheeriest grin and drops an arm on my shoulder. We are both grateful to be alive, and to get a breather. For, as much as we'd both like to bring this slaver to action, we know what the expense, in blood, could be.

On the other hand, the midshipmen on deck are heart-sick—they want to fight. Just one year ago, I felt that way myself—aching for action.

But now, even before the powder clears, I want no more of it. I think of the cool highlands of Jamaica, where the swallow-tailed doctor bird dips in and out of the trumpet flowers; everything is peaceful, and there is no more war.

*June 11, 1813*
*At anchor, Falmouth Harbor, midmorning*

We have put up and anchored down in a crawly fog. The queer feeling all of us have is that the guard ship knows we have scuttled their captives and have them onboard, and what they want now is to take their prisoners back and blow us out of the water in the process.

Are they out there in the grayish bunting now?

"How shall we prepare for action, sir?"

Captain Smythe, smacking his lips from the breakfast of burgoo, says to me, "Ever since I learned to walk on this dancing cork of a craft—I've given up guesswork. There's none to be done, or had, at sea."

I am pacing beside him, and the little cat's claws of fog are scattering playfully at our feet, and he, breakfast scarce past, is having a second repast of flasky grog.

He gives me an uncertain smile, then tugs off his officer's gold-buttoned coat, revealing his potbelly. "You see me, Tom, braced with my cutlass?"

"I see you, sir, as of course you see me."

"Then you well know that I am girded for action—flask notwithstanding. I beg you overlook this little sinful action, lad. Cannot help it, as I have had the shakes ever since I accepted this command, which is, I think, to be my last."

"Why do you say that, sir? You have plenty of life left in you."

"Life—but no desire, Tom." He stiffens as he says this, tucks away the flask, straightens up, and tucks his shirt in neat and officer-like.

In the prevalent, filching fog, stealing over everything—so that, even as he is before me, he is suddenly grayed away and lost—I seem to hear him as if from afar.

Then he stands again, in the clear. "Look to the *Kraaken,* Tom—for, between the two of us, she's yours more than mine. Look to—see to it that every man's posted proper, fog or no, and make sure they're pledged to their duty. Your ally Peter is aloft, aiding and abetting that poor dimwit Tailtackle. You've a world of friendship in that Peter; stay close to him, Tom."

"Sir, you're not leaving us, are you?"

Ignoring me, he goes on in this roughish monotone, punctuated by the rags of phantom fog. "Nedrick and his men and those crackshot slaves—have every man set to take aim. Mr. Yerk's below, at the moment, chomping on some cheese, but he'll soon be abovedecks—and then there's Mr. Catwell; make sure he packs his grapeshot for fearful effect. So, all should be well and ready, Tom. Let the fog do what it will. Those are your instructions. We will soon be under attack."

"You know this to be a fact, sir?"

"I know nothing but that."

"You have the gift for foreknowledge, sir."

"I have the gift for Madeira and rum, I am afraid. But you have the gift to be a fine officer. Of that I am also certain."

He salutes me—a little, small, almost halfhearted salute—and disappears to the privacy of his drink, I suppose.

So I am left with the fog as thick as cloth in the throat and like shards of glass when you swallow. The men hunker about like vapor-coated duppies, hugging their guns, and here it is, somber, soppy midday noon, dark as midnight on main.

I stare out into the molt light of day. My eyes see naught but the pale ghost faces of Johnny, Obed, and Tim.

*Still at anchor in the russet eve*

Out of the reddish gray gloom comes the sudden crack of a musket. I glance to the topmast and hear a terrible cry. Then the falling through rigging of one of our men. He hits the deck in a meaty *thump*. I rush through the gloom to find that it's crazy Tailtackle, shot through the heart. I cannot believe so loud and loose a man is now down and out. Looking at his surprised face, I see that he couldn't believe it, either.

Captain Smythe does not appear, but Peter is soon at my elbow. "Dey're back, Tom!"

"Where?"

I can see nothing but the ghostings of gray, shifting and tangling in rigging, and blotting out the fo'c'sle.

Then a breeze dampens my cheek, and a wind rises and sweeps the low-hanging clouds clear for a second, and I catch a glimpse of the guard ship cutting quietly out of the fog but a short distance from our anchored stern.

It is too late to draw anchor, or to prevent being raked.

So it is to be a sharpshooters' war—with our side and theirs firing full random, riddling both decks with shot. Glad am I that Sneezer's tied up in the gun room—I wouldn't want him on deck at this moment! Still, I can hear him howling for me.

"Thank God for the Coramantees," say I to Peter. We are crouched low on the fo'c'sle, while Mr. Nedrick, as ordered, holds his squad of sharpies tight. They pierce the fog banks tween ships, so that we hear the crack of arms, the spark of their guns. The confusion is twofold, for the attacker is but a few chains off our leeward side, and the wind picks up, sending fleeing, flying fog off our masts.

"Down with the helm, let her come round," I tell Peter, who is at the wheel. Mr. Yerk, flat as a flounder, is creeping across the deck, all cheesy mouthed. He is worming his way up as bullets chip a path in front of his face.

"There's the lucky wind. Sweep forward, Peter, and keep her there. Now get the other carronade to leeward, Mr. Catwell—that's it—now, blaze away while she's becalmed! Mr. Nedrick, take good aim, sir!"

I am barking orders before I can think them.

We are right now across her stern, having turned slowly round. Her spanker boom is now within yards of us.

What fortunate piloting from Peter, what fortuitous winds! Yet the dire brig's pouring shot from her rigging, her poop and cabin windows. Meanwhile, the splinters are whistling all round. However, we are still athwart her stern and hitting her fairly well with both cannon and musket.

For the first time, she's fully in the clearing. I see right well those reckless stars and stripes of that detestable American flag. I also see the hidden men among the masts, and the continual puffs of smoke from the shrouded sharpies that are killing our men, starboard and aft.

"There goes her main-topmast," cheers Captain Smythe. He has popped up like a gopher, unflasked and unshirted, and is now in the thick of it. A loud chorus goes up from Nedrick's and Catwell's men. "Pepper her while she's blinded and confused!" Captain Smythe hollers, waving his fist.

"Her flag's coming down, sir," states Mr. Yerk.

"Good work, lads," Captain Smythe says, swaggering. He crows out, "There it goes, the American stripes, dropping into the sea like a casualty of war."

Deflated, it flops down, and the mast from which it clapped is down, too, but a yard from where I stand is Tailtackle, eyes staring, heart stopped by an American bullet. For some reason this death really cuts me to the quick—well, he was so noisy and full of life, one couldn't imagine him ever dying. Especially after his aerial act in the channel. But there he is, the noise all punched out of him . . . forever.

Captain Smythe is reeling from his flask. If he sees Tailtackle, it is not noticeable. "Glorious, Tom, we've shot away the weather fore-topsail sheet. No way the rotters can get away from us now. Keep up your fire, Mr. Nedrick. Mr. Catwell, the same." He is conducting them, hither and yon, naked from the waist up and wearing his wig sideways.

In the fo'c'sle, standing side by side with him, I, despite Tailtackle lying there, feel a rush of pride. My cheeks burn. The thing is, I recall just such an undaunted moment with Obed. How it felt when the shot parted our hair and not one bullet scratched our skin and how we escaped sudden death together under withering fire.

I watch the brig as two Americans lie down upon the larboard fore-yardarm. They're desperately trying to splice the sheet, getting the clew of the fore-topsail down to the yard. If they should succeed in this, the brig could fetch away, if a wind should favor them. Anything can happen, anything at all.

"Have they a joker's wild chance, do you think, Tom?" Captain Smythe asks. "What goes up there, anyway?"

"A patching effort, sir. If we can but bring them down at their labor, the day will be ours."

The largest of the Africans, a man large enough to be a giant, is one Geronimo Hercules. He's in position for the shot, but he's looking the other way. Dropping off the fo'c'sle, I make a run for the larboard bulwark, close to the taffrail. Here are Bulla and two others. Finally, I catch up to Geronimo Hercules.

"Do you see those canvas splicers up top? Mark them well and shoot them down," I tell him.

He turns toward me with all the equanimity of his name, and his great, animated face burns with pleasure.

"Dem up dere on de end of de long stick?" His hypnotic gold brown eyes peer deeply into mine.

"Yes, the ones on the yardarm."

A sudden clattering of shot proves that our position's been spotted. And now they are throwing random loads of grape our way. I hunch down, making myself flat and small.

A chunk of grape whines at my ear. I feel a burn. Looking at my arm, I see there's a row of spines going all the way to my shoulder. I grit my teeth in pain and watch Hercules take aim. The powder from the brig is so close, it's actually burning our eyes, making them water.

Through blinding tears, I see the devils up there on the larboard fore-yardarm—a stick it is, indeed!—"Down with them, Hercules," I say through clenched teeth because of the splinters. A cannon burst springs our rigging, and it whips in the air.

Hercules stands out largely even when he is kneeling.

"Can you get down lower?" I ask as he prepares himself, balancing on one knee, the other foot bolstered down flat, and his great head cradled against the gun stock.

Ignoring my comment, he replies very coolly, "Tell de mon have ready me next one." He refers to the reload man tween-decks and the passing of new muskets up and out the hatch. Hercules now sights, fires, drops one man. Then the fellow to his rear. Finally, the third, and all three drop into the drink and sink so rapidly, they leave no stain on the surface of the sea. Hercules, the master marksman, is better at warcraft than even Mr. Nedrick.

I clap Hercules on the back, and it feels like I am congratulating a mountain. He smiles, briefly, then his face goes hard again. So I crawl back to Captain Smythe and report the news. Proud of my part in it, I expect a tiny prattle of praise, yet it doesn't come. Instead, Captain turns to Mr. Yerk. "Put the helm up and lay the ship alongside—they're done shooting for the day—stand by with the grapplings—one round the backstay—the other through the chain plate there—so—you have it!"

So now we are hooked up to our enemy, who is roundly and soundly defeated, so far as we can tell.

I am so boiling over from the sense of victory. Seizing the moment, I shout, "Boarders, follow me!" and I jump into the boarding netting and make for the deck of the American brig. My pistol's drawn, and my sword's naked. Amazingly, the broken enemy rallies once more. Some of those in the net with me are caught in a volley of fire. The net strings sing and ping and come undone. In spite of this, several of us struggle across to their quarterdeck.

About forty American fighting men await us on the brig. They are a very determined front, especially since their rear-guard sharpies are well armed and so well hidden, we can't even see them. Hercules' shadow falls over me; and he and I fire our pistols at the same time. In back of us, Nedrick's men perfume the air with smoke. Windblown in our direction, momentarily, it shrouds us, making our eyes tear. My pistol bullet cloves one man while another rushes me—I suppose he sees my gold-shouldered coat. With my eyes still blurry I cannot focus well on the rascal, so he cuts me just at the collar. A pinch, a painful one, which feels like cold water is trickling down my side.

There is no time to think, only time to react. Dropping my empty pistol, I raise my sword and clang hard against the opposing blade. In spite of the splinters lodged in my right arm and my new wound, I feel no pain, but we are all entangled—a great knot of boarders and resisters.

Now I hear hornets at my ear—grape from aloft. My sword arm works independently of me, having been trained by my father and the Navy, and it upholds my wounded body, and rescues it. In truth, I jab my enemy twice for his once. Then Peter, my savior, appears with a boarding pike and sends the fellow sprawling.

I turn, weakly, to thank him for saving my life, but he's gone into another whirlpool of men. I am left standing trying to catch my breath, leaning forward, hands on knees. The Americans have rallied, hard and fast but not for glory—for their very lives. I think they know we have them, but they keep rising up and licking us down and pushing us back. Then, most troublesome, they are besting us.

Out of the corner of my fighting eye, I see Hercules, bare

knuckled, battering down any and all within the parameter of his fists. He has gone all the way up the brig's bows, bashing down Americans and throwing them in the sea.

All at once, a discharge of grape crashes through the bridle port of the brig, killing some more of our men. I have strength left, and wounded though I am, I fall into the field of action with renewed fury. In my ears I hear a hundred chinking hammers jamming down a road of stones, and all the while men are skidding in their own blood.

Ahead of me, head-rammer Hercules presses on, living up to his name and throwing men up over his head like stalks of corn, so that they fall before him. Where he goes, death is certain—it seems to me no one can touch him.

Now there is fire down the hatchway; our men have lobbed some explosive shot down the hole to rout the enemy out, and it has caught the magazine on fire.

The brig is going to blow, and the Americans are jumping off the bowsprit into the sea as we British turn and run for the boarding net.

"Get back, men," Captain Smythe is baying, and we're scraping over the netting even as he speaks and the abandoned brig surges into a riot of flames. Most of the Americans are swimming ashore. Billows of black smoke roll up out of that fore-hatchway. I can feel the tremor before the blow—it's like an earthquake. Then I hear someone say, "We're going to be blown to onions." I slip and scramble, falling onto the deck of the *Kraaken,* but I'm thinking as I'm scrambling, That man means smithereens, not onions!

*Falmouth Harbor, eventide*

As soon as my feet find the deck of the *Kraaken,* my rubber legs buckle, and Peter Mangrove, faithful as ever, catches me and bears me up, and the two of us, hazy eyed, watch the smoldery smoke rise into a pillar of darkness from the fore-hatchway of the doomed guard ship.

A crimson flame scampers up the American sails and eats furiously at the rigging while dropping ashen banners in its burny wake. Whereupon, the fire spreads to every part of the gear aloft, and the other element, the sea, strives for equal mastery of destruction. She settles down by the head, and then we hear the water rush in like a millstream.

Still, the fire increases, and as we are pulling away from our fetter lines, to get free of this imminent danger, the cannons go off as they get biliously heated, hurling shards of iron in all directions, and the brig gives a sudden heel and starts to go down with a heavy lurch, head foremost, into the smoke-fazed, fog-curled sun.

I am all but hanging off Peter's shoulder, watching.

Drained from loss of blood—neck and arm—I have my last smudgy sight of the brig as the dun wreaths burst from her belly and she heaves and shudders once more—and sinks.

Glowing like an amethyst in the sun, the brig lights up one last time amid the smoke and ruin of the day, and so goes down into the sea with her night candles, so to say, brightening the fathoms.

"What is left of her?" I ask Peter, for my eyes—teared and tired from the acrid smoke—are tightly shut.

"Nuttin'," he replies.

I can hear Mr. Jigmaree going about amid the groans of our wounded, tending to them.

When I open my eyes next, I am being borne up by Peter, and Mr. Jigmaree is ringing my neck with swathes of cotton cloth; and I am wrapp't tighter than a golden chicken on All Saints' Day.

I find myself sitting naked in a wading tub. It is dank and dewy with my own oozy blood. All in all, some thirty stitches I've taken and I would like to think I bear them well, between some medicinal swallows of dark rum, and Peter is saying, "Tom, her gone from still water, gone down; an' all roun' de dark ripple weh she go, dem swim an' dem bubble rise up oveh de masthead, an' den it be silent as de grave, and dere is no more fi say."

I blink dazedly as Mr. Jigmaree, darning needle darting, knots my wound and sponges me clean. "The rascal nicked you right over the collarbone," he says through his blood-flecked spectacles. "His blade glanced, then went up a ways, clipping your neck. Now I must see about these splinter nicks on your arm."

Glancing along my right arm, from shoulder to wrist, I see a path of little ruby red tracks, as if a centipede had run a blood-footed race there. Then I remember the splinters that were attached to me before we boarded the brig; after the initial pain, I hadn't paid them any mind.

"A pretty-pretty sugar plum, dat wound," Peter remarks.

I nod sleepily as Mr. Jigmaree continues to swab me clean. I am sore all over and swimmy from the loss of blood. But, overall, I am anxious to know how it went at the end when I temporarily lost my sight.

Peter explains that the escapees have swum for Falmouth shore, where, he says, they shall soon be rounded up like loose cattle, one stray beast at a time.

Somehow, he gets me out of that dire pinkish tub and onto my wobbly feet and then into my bloodstained trousers. This is all I remember, for then I am carried off hence to my hammock, where I awaken and find my head clear enough to scribble some more—I have to write when I can, lest I forget.

After this, I get a touch of the old fever.

Peter stays near, and from time to time I hear him saying, "Dere, now, Tom," as he cools my face with a cloth. All the while, I feel Sneezer's hot breath near my face and him licking me all about my wounds.

I drop into a sickish sleep.

And dream of Jenkins, my old nemesis aboard the *Bream.* He is chasing me through a ruined building, a great house full of water, and I am sinking with his hands clutched to my throat, and then I am suddenly awakened to the stifling gun room night . . . and it's Sneezer lolloping me with licks as before.

*June 14, 1813*
*Falmouth Town, three days after*

When I wake, it's Captain Smythe at my side telling me to get dressed and come ashore, for there's work to do. "Tom, if your meager neck wasn't so hard and bony, that fellow might've severed your top," he jokes.

"Well, I am nicely coopered now," I say, sitting up in my hammock.

"How do you feel, lad?"

"Stiffish, but ready to take command, if you wish."

"Command? Nonsense. But we do have a bit of an assignment for you, if you're up to it, Tom."

I hear his ten-league boots creak off and his sword hilt clinking, and then I try standing, but everything is moving. I know we are anchored in close to shore, so it has to be me that is swaying to and fro. Anyway, I dress myself, slow and picky as an old maid, and follow Captain Smythe to his cabin.

There he informs me that I have a message awaiting me from no less than the mayor of Falmouth.

"What could he possibly want of me, sir?"

"I believe he has a letter for you. Can you walk apace?"

"Of course."

"Then why don't you and Peter and Sneezer get a breath of fresh air and go fetch that letter?" He takes a little snort of snuff and settles into his chair with a loud sigh.

Thus do I go off the ship and into town, where we are met by a short, priggish little man who introduces himself as the mayor of Falmouth.

"Sir," he says, straight off, "our entire village is indebted to you for your brave action."

To which I say, "It was nothing."

Whereupon he puts in, "Well, it was *something,* for I see you are twice wounded, sir."

As we speak, we are walking under the shade of the coconut palms and going toward an inn just ahead. The overdressed little mayor waxes on. "Why," says he, "won't our government stop this nefarious trade?"

"You mean the slave trade," I add.

"Quite so," agrees the mayor.

He stops in front of a wooden sign, THE FIGHTING COCKEREL, just as an oxcart rumbles past.

"Sir," says the mayor, tugging my sleeve, "the question is not the iniquity of the program, but how, in fact, we should break it down. Do we throw out the *entire* economy, then?"

"Better that, sir, than to break the backs of the men who are in service of it. As I see it, there must be an alternate way of harvesting sugar and making rum."

Peter, edging himself into the conversation, nods his agreement. "Mek all de planter dem wuk, too," he suggests dryly.

The mayor raises his eyebrows. "Don't go so far," he exclaims. "You can't throw the baby out with the bathwater. But I do see your point."

"Why not?" Peter grins impishly. "Trow de baby off inna de bush and him be better off fi dat."

"These are *not* my sentiments," the mayor contends. "We must ease ourselves out of this entanglement, not abandon it altogether. That would ruin the planters."

"I thought they were the misbegotten sons of the rich, anyway," I tell him quite frankly, but he frowns at me and at Peter all the more. Oh, how I loathe these stuffed-shirt landed appointees whose stipend from home grants them everything but a brain. And, anyway, I am feeling a little stiff-necked myself and would like a bit of refreshment for myself and Peter, so I hasten to his delivery of my letter, which, forthwith, he hands over very agreeably, thanking us once again for our contribution to the safety of the island.

"Him a bag-o-wind," Peter says, chuckling as the puffy little mayor trots off on some other pressing errand. This leaves us to have a pleasant cool drink under the bricked arches of the old inn.

I open the letter, which has the red wax seal from Cinnamon Hill plantation.

*My dear Mr. Cringle,*

*I am much the better for the recent news—brought by one of our men who was in Falmouth when the American ship was scuttled. We have heard nothing further, but I trust that you are all right and that this finds you in the best of health. Please be advised that we lost twelve of our best slaves. They were taken off our plantation by pirates of the worst kind. Should they turn up on one of your captured ships, we will anticipate their immediate return. We have posted a reward for said slaves, and of course you and your captain would be the recipient. Do stay well away from the main roads because, we are told, these American rascals seem to be spread out at all points of the compass.*

*I am your steadfast friend,*

*Mr. A. Cranston, Esq.*

*Cinnamon Hill*

"So Tom, wha' gwan?" Peter asks when I put down the letter.

But before I can reveal the contents of the letter, I glance up from my pewter mug and catch sight of an all too familiar face. Seeing this face does me a bad turn—for there, dead ahead, sitting at a table by the bar is none other than Mr. Jenkins, and a rowdier-looking ragamuffin you never saw! His face, from where I am peering, looks askew, as if he'd had a terrible accident. Well, that must have been near-death . . . because he was one of those supposed to be dead when the *Bream* went down. And here he is, alive and well, and feisty as a rooster.

Fortunately, the blackguard doesn't see me at all; he is turned slightly to one side. Nor can I see the fellow he is conferring with in low tones, both of their heads half in shadow. My heart is fluttering like a caged bird. With much dispatch, I excuse myself, and while giving Peter the eye, I pay for our drinks and we leave expeditiously. Out in the hot glare of the cobbled street, it is a while before I can even get a proper breath. The sight of that man, looking like a mad egg with a stocking cap, his close-set eyes staring ahead of him, I am sure he did not see me—looking at that other man, whoever he might be.

"Did you see him, Peter?" I ask when we are well away from the Fighting Cockerel.

"Me see him all de while," Peter answers with a hard edge to his voice.

"My throat went dry when I laid eyes on him."

"Gone pirate, him has," Peter says.

"How do you know?"

"Dis." He thrusts a crumpled piece of paper into my hands. It's a handbill.

"Where did you get this, Peter?"

"Me find it just now on dat tree over yonder."

"I didn't see you fetch it. I guess I am in a daze."

I stare at the sunken face of my old nemesis. Decked out in printer's ink, he looks much the same, except the disfigurement I saw at the inn appears as a bad burn in the heavily inked, very crude drawing. Seeing him surface on paper causes my heart to beat hard again, and I wonder—Am I such a coward that this man can inflict such fear in me?

"The handbill says the man's name is Three-Fingered Jack. There's no other alias given."

"Name change, man stay de same," says Peter resolutely.

Back on the *Kraaken* I tell Captain Smythe there are two important matters we must discuss. Ale-eyed and sweaty, the captain is all stretched out in his hammock with his boots kicked off, his shirt undone. "Warm day, Tom," he says listlessly when I show him the handbill. He gives it a cursory stare and offers it back to me. "Do you really think Jenkins is somehow messed up in this affair of ours? I mean, he's on our official roster as dead, and this bloke's called Three-Fingered Jack."

"Would he be so bold as to show up in a public place?" I ask.

"A dead man?" Captain Smythe wiggles his toes and stretches.

"Dead or alive, he's fearless of authority."

Finding an apple in the fold of the hammock, Captain Smythe crunches into it, then says, "No pirate worth his salt fears the Navy on dry land. Besides, did you recognize him *positively?* Or do you just *think* you saw him?"

At this, I'm taken aback. "Do you doubt my vision, sir?"

"Onboard ship, no. On land, it's another thing. You said he was in the darkish depths of the inn, was he not?"

"I suppose."

Peter scratches his head. "I saw him, too, sir."

"I don't doubt that you both *thought* you saw him. But this man *could* be someone else. His name doesn't have the same ring, does it? What is the other matter you wished to speak to me about?"

I then give him Mr. Cranston's letter, and he reads it with one eye blinked shut and holding the paper close to his nose. "Very well, then, Tom, I am going to send you and Peter the roundabout way with those slaves. You can go over the hills and to the south, and from there you can easily get to Cinnamon Hill. It's off the beaten path, but therefore safe as can be. I'll oversee the hauling off of the anchored-down slave ship and that brawly bear of yours, too. Do we have an understanding?"

I give him a weak salute with my slinged-up right hand. He's snoring before I reach the door.

*June 15, 1813*
*Near the Millbrae River*

So now I have orders to journey up the Millbrae River all the way to the juncture of the road at Maroontown. Thence, we go down the mountain to Port Royal. If we follow said route, it is anticipated by Captain Smythe that we'll meet no wayfarers. The great concern is that we should avoid the lot just escaped from the brig that we dispatched—American pirates, some fifteen of them, who jumped from the bows and got away. Night cloaked them when they hit the beach, and they scattered like rats.

We think they'll go back to Cinnamon Hill for another try at capturing more slaves; or they'll attempt to seize back the men they lost. We're to confuse them by following the Millbrae through some of the roughest jungle the island has to offer.

It's deucedly hot; the air's thick as porridge. The soreness in my neck's irksome, but so it goes.

One of the men with Hercules sees a field full of john-crow vultures settling like black ashes among the arms of a tuna cactus. On close inspection we find the limp, dead body of a mongrel dog with its mouth tied shut by a bandanna such as pirates wear. The poor animal was strung up and tied to the cactus very crudely with rope. Who would do such a thing?

The Africans are all saying it is obeah, that form of dark

magic or sorcery wherein people vanish, turn fool, and walk into the jungles, openmouthed and mad. A sign to haunt us on our way, and Peter gives me no end of commentary on it—the practice of obeah, a stronger force than a hurricane, as he puts it. One of the Africans, a man named Barra, gets out his obeah-warding-off necklace. "Juju," he confides when I ask him what all the wooden beads are about.

"Dat mean good magic," Peter explains. Barra, whom I have already begun to like, nods and grins along with his partner, Bulla.

The sky is adazzle with the shuddering john-crows. We drive them off and untie the dead dog and put him to rest with pick and shovel. Meanwhile, the john-crows pitch about in the palms with grand undertaker's wings and their naked heads.

Sneezer hasn't the disdain for the dead that I have and he would gladly sniff of the corpse, but I hold on to his collar and don't let him get near. It's a hard image to shake: that of the bandanna-muzzled dog, strung out like a crucified man on the tree of cactus. "Do you think it has anything to do with Jenkins?" I ask Peter as the dog's grave is tamped down by Barra and Bulla.

"Axe me no question, me tell you no lie," Peter says evasively, smiling.

"Come, Peter, I know you have some thoughts on this."

"Wha me tink, nuh set your mind at ease, Tom."

By which, I conclude, that Peter sees that dead dog as a kind of warning. The signature of something evil.

*Marching along by the Millbrae, later that day*

I sit upon a balky little donkey while Peter is astride a rawboned mule. Sneezer tramps between us, tongue lolling. Poor dog, his heavy, black, curly hair is no bargain in this hot sunlight.

Behind us is a train of mules, laden with packs filled with victuals. In back of them is the line of unshackled slaves, who are singing as they walk along this red road in the hot summer sun.

All the way in back, having rear coverage, are our sharp marksman, Mr. Nedrick, and our great cannoneer, Mr. Catwell. All move along the Millbrae, the lazy, little green stream that comes down out of Cockpit Country. This is the

region famed for its grayish spires and cliffs and its vast vegetative green depths.

My stitches itch in the heat, so I unburden myself of the bandage. Perhaps the air may do them some good. Now we move up into the first hills outside of Falmouth. Atop the promontories, we spy some old ruined sugar plantations. Scattered about, hither and thither, are the fragments of broken-down sugarhouses, half-sunk into the overgrown fields. After a while, the road narrows and grows green in the middle, as the topknot of grass widens—and after a little while, it is a narrow bridle path we're on and it spools away into the bush.

I write, as usual, catch-as-catch-can. On donkeyback. Except for the constant bumps, I am at no loss for words. But now—as I scribble—the path starts to ascend, and we leave the loamed, steamy lowlands. Here in the higher country, the air is colder and thinner at every turn.

The Africans are led in song by Hercules. It's a chant of sorts that measures their pace and seems to lighten their load—so Peter says.

I am thinking that I hardly know them. And yet their faces seem so familiar. Barra has a long, underslung jaw like a barracuda on the prowl. I am told he is a ferocious fighter and a good man to have on your side. I ask him what he sees out there in the bush, for his eyes are always peering out at things.

He walks alongside my donkey. "Me see same as you, Meester Creengle."

"I doubt that, for I see only what is in front of my face."

His open mouth leers, breaking into a droopy grin.

"What's so funny?"

"You tink me see trew tree an' stone."

I chuckle—it is so. I do think he can pierce through the jungle's gloom, but he makes me laugh at myself for this.

"Me see wha me *need* fi see, Meester Creengle. But dat be 'nuff."

"It's good enough for *me*," I tell him. Then he gives me a searching look that holds my eyes for a moment. "What?" I ask him.

"Yuh de mon wid de eye dem," he says admiringly. "Dem seh you haff eagle eye, fi true."

"Is that so?" I shrug. But his compliment warms my heart. By "dem" he means his people, the Africans, and I am more than a little proud to be known for something other than my youth or my belittling height.

"I understand how Barra got his nickname, but how did Bulla get his?"

"Him kotch dat name," Peter tells me, "'cause him haffa eat bulla bread all de while." That is the cheap flour and molasses bread. Curiously, there's nothing the least bit fat about Bulla; he's lean as a plank.

The paunchy one's named Pawnzo. He's got a belly on him, all right, and one that runs a close second to Captain Smythe's, if there were ever a contest. But I must say, Pawnzo, though older, moves like a man half the captain's age. He's frosty on the head and fast on the feet and whenever he sees me, he calls me Colonel. "I'm First Lieutenant Cringle," I tell him, but after I ride past, he says, "Awright, Colonel Creengle." When I swivel around to look at his face, he's nodding and blinking. "Yah sah, Colonel Creengle, saah." Smiling to himself—but not disrespectfully, I observe, just in his funny, personable way. I'd like, if possible, to know more of these men, but some are so withdrawn, it doesn't seem possible. The color of my skin and my rank conspire to make any friendliness suspicious to them, I'm afraid.

Presently, we're completely out of the sun, deep into the heart of the forest. The bridle path disappears into a shady clump of bamboo that turns into a tunnel through which we wind our way in the coolness thereof.

*Along the Millbrae, noon*

We repair to the cool banks of the Millbrae to water our animals and ourselves. While at rest, I put pen to paper.

Sneezer is the first to get wet; he jumps into a clear pool, scattering silver minnows in all directions. Then, after barking and biting the water, he paddles to shore and rolls over in the papyrus. He gets up, after the show—and wiggling the tippy point of his tail, sends rainbows off it. Then he heaves himself down again, kicking his heels at the sky.

Next, the donkeys are braying, and the mules are, too. They all gather under a flowering tulip tree and nip at one another's ears and chew away at the groundwood saplings.

Our dinner is made up mainly by Hercules, Pawnzo, and Bulla. (I notice them doing a fair amount of sampling, too.) The meal consists of things from our packs. I refer, all in all, to johnnycake, roasted breadfruit, baked ring-necked dove (this last was brought down by a stone thrown unwaveringly by Barra), and some boiled yam. This is the best meal we've had in months. After supper, I order a night watch of sorts. For though it's broad day outside the forest, within it's darkish night—and a good time to catch a puss-nap, as they say. So some of us get some sleep while the rest stay on watch.

I am watching the lone man called Geechee. Dressed in old, soiled trousers with no shirt, he, unlike the other Africans, keeps entirely to himself. When I ask Peter why this is, he answers that *geechee,* in patois, means "ghost" or "spirit," and that this fellow came from the Carolinas, where he was badly mistreated. His eyes seem to turn within. This is also true of Picky, Maubie, and Mafeena, who keep to themselves and have little to say.

"How goes it, Peter?" I ask.

"Me nuh sleepy, Tom," Peter says, coming over to me. He's scanning the upper reaches of the bamboo.

"You think Jenkins is out there?"

"Me tink so."

"We have with us the best marksmen in the Caribbean."

He nods, eyes glued to the uppermost leaves. "You see dem bamboo?"

"Beautiful trees," say I.

"Me see a man once . . . cut a fort outta dem tree. Can use bamboo fe mek a cannon, too."

The bamboo grove cries in the June wind, buffeting us with a beautiful breeze.

"Should we check around, then, Peter?"

"Cha!" he scorns. "Dat bamboo be honderd chain across—you can't see trew it. You can't cut trew it! But who know what on de other side of it?"

The bamboo, as if agreeing with him, creaks loudly, chafing at the joints and reminding us that we're kind of locked up in a prison of green vertical bars.

"Me just watch, Tom. Even when dere is nuttin' fi see."

He is right. Whatever he feels, I feel, too. The wind dives again, making the prison walls shudder. I cannot but think that this is my first real command, my first test of manhood on the land; and if my rank and judgment do not uphold me here—what shall? The wary eyes of Peter do not close; thank God for him!

For, soon, my eyelids grow heavy in the dark of noon. And against my will, standing and leaning against the bamboo jail walls, I fall dead asleep.

*By the Millbrae, moonrise*

I have a fevery dream in which Jenkins is trying to suffocate me with my officer's coat. His fingers are like claws close on my neck. His face is all burned—the way it was in the handbill, ratty eyed and burny looking.

I am awake, my back to the bamboo, still standing.

The sparkle of water, the gleam of moonbeam. Webs of silver all around us. Am I still adream?

I see Jenkins, his burned face thrust before me.

I blink. He is gone.

Peter, who seems not to have moved, is still staring straight ahead. He hands me a tin cup, saying, "Some coffee, Tom."

I take the hot cup; it warms my shaking hands—and I realize I have been asleep for hours. Looking around, I see that the Africans have repacked our stores. They are filling our canteens in the stream. Through the moonlit silence, a lone bird makes its melancholy call.

A *chick-mon-chick* bird, the Jamaican bird of death.

"You hear dat?" Peter asks.

I nod, and he says despairingly, "Bad luck bird, dat."

I touch my tender neck, still prickly and hot.

Soon we are on our journey heading up the bridle path that leads through the hollow of bamboo. The bank of the river, swathed in the softest moonglow, bubbles pleasantly. Peter edges up to me on his little beast, whose breath fairly steams from its nostrils—the higher we go, the colder it gets.

"You see the moonlight sleeping on that bank?" I whisper to Peter.

He answers, "Me nuh know what sleeps dere, Tom, but me *know* what don't sleep up dere."

"What do you mean?"

He gestures at the cliff to our left. I follow his eye and see, with a start, a half-naked figure of a man with an enormous head. He, or it, is kneeling on one knee. He is etched against the sky, and I see him move. (What a fool I have been, in a drowse whilst we are in danger!)

Then comes the click of a carabine lock. It is plain and audible set against the sounds of the tree frogs. Still, the line of men and mules goes patiently, stubbornly, up the ravine. I ask Peter if he thinks the man on the bluff had anything to do with the dead dog, the obeah sign. He shrugs, and says, "Me find a next one."

"What?"

"Back inna de bamboo, me find dis."

He opens a torn piece of cloth; inside of this is a dog's foot severed from the leg.

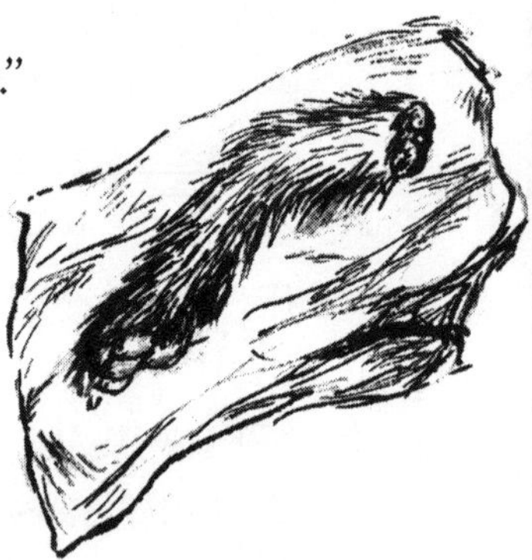

"Get rid of that," I tell him.

He pitches it into the dark. Sneezer sneezes; a shiver goes up my spine.

In truth, I should like to call a halt—the figure and the dog's foot strike a chill into my heart. But I am loath to do it, for stopping would make us that much more vulnerable. Withdrawing my pistol from my belt, I drop softly from my wooden saddle and get into a crouch. Peter does the same. I feel his hand on my shoulder. He puts his first finger to his lips and shakes his head, warning me not to say or do anything. Sneezer presses my right shoulder. He is panting, drooling, and growling between breaths. Some of his saliva spatters my neck. He is pointing as at a duck shoot, his great, shaggy shape tilting at the haunted figure on the cliff.

The tall man—and he evidently is one—keeps apace of our line, moving slowly, striding on the high rocks. He is well positioned: He can see all that fills the lighted ravine. We are his; he owns us—by sight. As for our owning him, well, he fades in and out of sight as our train continues on with the sound of the donkeys' unshod feet and the mules' iron-shod hooves chipping the stony turf.

Down by the Millbrae, the moonvale flickers on the dun ground, and a night wind lifts the leaves. In a twinkling, my eye sees three dark shapes advance from the pearly stream. Behind these are gathered more shadows, all of them massing in the ferns. Muskets, too, poking out of the bracken.

I check to see if my pistol is primed, and seeing that it is, I give Peter the command: "Tell all we're being attacked!" With the palm of my left hand, I feel the curved walnut handle of my second pistol; that, too, is primed and ready.

So here are we, in the sights of two evils—one above, many below. The animals grunt, lurch, stop. I listen as the weight shifts on their heavily burdened backs. We all stand stock-still—quiet people and stamping, hard-breathing animals. Yet every man among us is alerted, and armed. The man on the ridge is fixed just like we are, and now I notice his long gun standing upright like a spear.

Above the stamp of hooves, I bring back the hammers of my pistols. At which I hear other iron clicks in the fern brake; and by the riverside, more hammers cocking.

They must be a militia down there, I think, as the shadows keep multiplying. My heart is hammering, my mouth dry. The very trees draw a solemn breath. Then Mr. Nedrick, on foot and ducking down by the ferns, comes swiftly up to me. "If that rooftop laddie," he says, all out of breath, "means evil, I shall nick him in the bud."

I nod. "What of those down in the dell?" I whisper.

"Hercules has them covered," he replies softly.

"Catwell?"

"Two muskets, one in either hand."

I look about and see him, all stout and starkish to my eye, but well hidden from the vantage of the stream.

These men, I know, are geniuses at tactics. I am thankful to have them, but where, I wonder, is Peter? I turn and see that while I have been conversing with Mr. Nedrick, he has crawled all the way up to that escarpment. He is right beneath the shadow on the cliff.

In a trice, I see him hoist himself up and join the man.

Then I am drawn away by an unfamiliar sound down by the Millbrae: A spur jingles. I had never thought of that, for some reason—the pirates having horses!

"Catastrophe awaits the beggars," Nedrick whispers to me. Then he slips off, heading downward, slipping invisibly through the ferns. I follow in his wake, when, catching my boot against a rock . . . I take a plunge, muttering an oath under my breath . . . can I not do anything right? But as I fall hard, my right-hand pistol strikes ground and discharges with a puff-and-boom and a squirt of yellow flame.

All at once, the river's ablaze with gunfire. This draws

forth fire from both sides and from up top as well. Now three men by the river make a run at us. I see Mr. Nedrick flash upward, sight, and fire. Quickly, he picks one of them off. His second gun lights the night; a second pirate spills into the Millbrae and, like a sodden log, is swept easily downstream, heels up and head down.

"That's one," I say under my breath as I am reloading my pistol, jamming the wadding, spilling gunpowder. I taste the peppery burn on my upper lip as I wipe the sweat off with my sleeve. Sneezer, crouched at my side, is barking, but he won't attack until the fighting is close.

All at once, a bunch of wild, raveled men tear out of the bush.

I run at one of them and find myself face-to-face with a mustachioed, headbanded pirate, who reaches out and grabs both of my pistols. With a quick jerk, he pulls them away from me before I can even fire them. From the force of this forward action, I lose my balance and drop back on my hind end.

Sneezer, hiding all the while, springs at the pirate's throat. The pistols pop off, in succession, but Sneezer's growling and dragging of the man continue unabated, so I know that he's not been hit.

Now, as I rise, there are two pirates down in the brake firing from behind a log. One of our men—long-jawed Barra, I believe—closes in on them, firing from the side. His attack is backed up by a queer, whirling noise, as of a giant bee flexing its wings very rapidly. I look along our line and there is Hercules, making a frightful, weird noise with his throat.

The log men look all round to see what the deuce this is,

and Hercules, at leisure, sights and shoots them. They twist almost whimsically, like dancers, and kick back into the stream. I hear Hercules say, "Good target." And I wonder how he got so good with a long gun.

Sneezer is back at my side when a clear-sounding British voice resonates from the Millbrae. "Truce," it calls out. Then, "See here, we have no wish to hurt you. Submit and render up our slaves, which we rightfully bought at Cinnamon Hill."

"You could not prove that," say I.

"We have the bill of sale with us."

This is Jenkins talking. I would know his bass voice anywhere. No telling how many men he has with him—I can't see them. Nor can I see him—just hear him.

Our men are waiting for me to answer.

I get up out of the ferns. "Stand clear, Jenkins," I tell him, "as I do."

Jenkins, the man himself, comes boldly out of the shadows. "All right," he calls. "But my name now is Three-Fingered Jack. So, is that you then, Tom?"

"How did you guess?"

"Who else is the size of a garden midget?"

A volley of guffaws on his side of the Millbrae.

I lower my voice as much as I am able, and say strongly, "All right, Two-Finger, if that's who you wish to be."

"Three-Finger," he corrects.

"What's one or more fingers among friends, now, Jack?"

A belly laugh from Hercules. Bless him for that. Then, silence. The river's voice, purling along, nothing else.

I continue: "You should know that there is a law governing

the trafficking of slaves. But do you know there's a handsome price on that waxed-up head of yours, and no amount of dog's paws is going to save you?"

"Nor will you have the power to save that mutt of yours, talking to me this way, Tiny Tom. We bought these men and I have the document to prove it." His voice, reined in, so to say, rumbles with menace.

"The buying and selling of slaves—the whole thing's been shut down by order of Parliament. And you're a wanted man, *Mr. Jenkins.*" I say this clear as can be through the moony prism of the glen, and to my way of thinking, there is a certain power in my speech. Forthwith, Jenkins drops his paper in the stream and steps backward into the pewtery leaves of the riverbank.

I can see him well in his queerly cut tight pants, his round blue jacket and epaulets, his stocking cap. In the moonlight his face looks skinned, dark sockets for eyeholes, sunken cheeks.

His head is like a talking skull, suspended in the silvery light; the leaves have erased the rest of him.

A horse's cough arises from the rushes where his reserves—on horseback—prepare to charge; I can feel this coming as readily as the presence of a storm. To Nedrick, who is close to my elbow, I say, "Don't shoot till they are midway of the stream."

Hercules answers with a grunt on my left.

Sneezer growls.

The air's full of ominous, cold clicks.

Then, of a sudden, the muskets, long knives, cutlasses, and guns come a-gleaming and a-rattling out of the thickets f the Millbrae, and the charge crashes—not into the water, but to one side of it, along the bank. Jenkins and some thirty pirates on horseback breach the water and clatter across the glittery sandbar. They're in our midst before we can answer their charge with more than a few shots.

Hercules' African throat-chant is like a bagpipe drone—a call to fight to the death—but I hear it only when I am not clashing my sword and when he is reaching for his reload gun. For the moment, with me, there is no reason but reflex. I know my life is on the line.

I am clashing with a swordsman on horseback. Sneezer is after the animal's legs, and it is jolting sideways, upsetting its rider. I take advantage of this with a long, deep thrust. The rider clutches his ribs, and folds. His mount shies, whinnies, whirls, and runs off with him.

I raise my blade to another pirate on horseback, but the thump of Mr. Nedrick's gun brightens the night, and his grapeshot flips the fellow backward like an acrobat. He rolls downhill, disappearing in the reeds.

In the space of a moment, Mr. Nedrick and I retreat behind our donkeys. He rests a reload gun given him by Pawnzo on the saddlebow of his donkey. Cradling cheek to stock, Mr. Nedrick says with his usual ease, "Let 'em come, Mr. Cringle."

Above the cliff, I hear the boom of two more marksmen; quick glance and I see it is Peter and the tall mystery man firing down with perfect precision—one firing, one loading. Each shot plumps into bone, and another pirate drops down the vale. A cutlass man comes round where I am catching my breath. And there, backed against my donkey, I bang steel with him. His blade sings near my head—I duck and feint doing what I do best, riposte and thrust. What I lack in strength, I make up for in speed. The trouble is, my right arm is sore, and slower than I would like. But I still catch the blackguard off guard. He swipes again—is that all he knows how to do?—and I counter with a slice upward, high and hard across his chest and chin.

I wonder at how easily I've overcome this man—then I see that it is all Sneezer's doing. The clever dog's bitten him from behind and drawn him backward at the same time I sliced forward. Yet no sooner is this over than another bloke takes his place. This is an old, tattered demon, his head bound right tight with that idiot's kerchief that all pirates love to gird themselves with.

He's at me in a trice—and then I see there are two of them, so that I'm feinting and fighting two clangers instead of one, but again, I have Sneezer, and he has them going round in circles, as they are stabbing wildly at him. I wonder he is not pierced when, suddenly, he takes hold of the old one's boot flaps. As the man takes a *swoosh* at Sneezer, I prick a hole in him from the side. Upon this deed he makes a seedy, resinous cough. Then he hobbles into the darkness, faintly moaning and calling someone's name.

Another pirate presses on, this one a real swordsman who doubtless knows the meaning of the word *style.* Several times he nearly skewers me, but I turn—and turn again the opposite way. Then I hear his sword point go *tock!*—into the wooden donkey saddle behind my left shoulder.

Once, he hones within a half inch of my slow right arm. I parry and strike his face with my hilt.

Stunned, he lets fall his weapon.

But, fumbling in his belt, comes up with a dirk. He lunges, low and at the level of my navel. I back up and slip beneath my donkey's belly, then pop up, bright and nimble, on the other side. Now the poor beast is between us like a bulwark. I take this opportunity to levy a long, loose, lazy-seeming arc.

He grabs his face with a shriek. I have sliced his forehead clean as a Virginia ham—and a thin fold of pink skin flaps over his eyes and blinds him. Groping blindly, his face red-sheeted in blood, the pirate bemoans the day. Then Sneezer hauls him off by the britches, so that he tumbles down the fern hill.

Round the moonlit circle, both sides are fighting furiously. Not to mention Peter on yon hill peppering the ranks of the pirates, dropping them one at a time while his secret second, the man on the ridge, does the same—the two of them, brother-fowlers on high, are dispatching pirates with great alacrity. Hercules and his men are likewise cracking pates and swinging staffs and musket stocks. There is no longer time to load or reload—it's all hand-to-hand now. Yet despite our smaller force and our unmounted condition, we seem to be getting the better of them. This gives rise to Jenkins's bitter cry, "Retreat, men, we're swept!"

The horsemen's turnabout is immediate. Hooves strike sparks as riders spur them back down the slope. A last crack of Peter's musket turns one reeling pirate to jelly in his saddle. Then, with an explosion of spray, the pirates crash through the Millbrae and are gone.

For a moment, their angry oaths fill the little glen. After which—with a boiling whinnying and stamping—the dread commotion fades into the bamboo silences of the forest until there is nothing left but our own hard fetching of breath.

I sit, all in a sweat, tugging off my soiled coat.

My right arm hangs all but useless, a limp thing. My neck wound, from the exertion, has begun to leak blood.

Sneezer's all over my face, cleansing me; good thing, too, as I am weeping with relief that the fight is over and we have won the day. No one sees the flood of tears he is licking away from my eyes.

Shortly thereafter, Peter appears, standing tall with his statuesque friend. Peter is singing, the way he used to do, making up a silly song about me:

*"Whether him live,*
*Whether him die,*
*Tom Creengle nevah know*
*De reason why!"*

This he repeats over and over, causing every one to cackle.

*June 16, 1813*
*On the bridle path to the Cockpit Country*

This morning I put pen to paper in order to say that we weathered the fight well. We can count seven of their fold dead. Of ours, the first man killed, an African slave named Mercy, is the only one who lost his life. The sadness I feel for this cannot be measured, for it was, and is, my command that got him killed.

The rest of us, however, are hale and hearty, though all are powder burned and purplish bruised, and pretty generally nicked about the edges from the savage fight. My neck hurts, my arm's sore, and the men can hardly walk upright without a groan, or without some little hitch of grief.

Still, a victory, I call it. A repulsion of an enemy far greater than us; and with seven of them gone to the hereafter and three floated off downstream, either dead or mortally wounded, we are unquestionably the winners.

I believe that Hercules is worthy of ten—so, too, is clever Peter Mangrove, and we mustn't forget Mr. Nedrick or Mr. Catwell. And then there is the tall, mystic man from the mountain. He, as it turns out, is an emissary, a Maroon warrior, sent to meet us.

The Maroons are well known in Jamaica for having fought against the Crown and having won their independence and the sanctity of their own preserve, that which is called Maroontown, the very place we are now heading for. The name comes from *cimarrón,* Spanish for "wild, unruly." This stranger is anything but that, a handsome man forged of black steel metal. Worthy of his mettle, too, I might add. Judging from our battle, I'd say he levies a stiff musket tariff.

The man's called Captain Cuffee. A clever fellow of rank sent to us by the great Cudjoe himself (more of him anon). The Maroons now fight for King George and honor him ever since their sovereignty was awarded some hundred years ago.

Anyhow, Captain Cuffee, after being introduced all round, takes leave of us with the following warning: "Watch de road, yuh cyaan tell wah a-gwan dere." So saying, he departs our company by promising to serve best while watching from afar. Cuffee offers Peter an abeng, a conch shell used to call from great distances. "Blow, an' listen fi me answer," he tells Peter, and then he slips off into the garlands of green.

I watch his great boarskin headpiece bobbing up and down as he ascends the ridge, where his dark body catches the sun once before he disappears.

I must say that I feel safer with him around.

Peter hangs the leather-slinged abeng over his shoulder, and we, after a small repast of bread, begin our trek toward the Cockpit Lands. Presently, we leave the Millbrae behind us; ahead lies uncertainty. In a while the bridle path turns into a gurgling streamlet, and the path is gone altogether. We refresh ourselves there, and Peter goes into our provisions. He passes round some jerk fish, smoky tasting and delicious. Mr. Nedrick delves into another deep basket and produces a bit of Scotch mutton Mr. Halsey gave us before we left Falmouth.

Thus do we rest whilst the waters leak out of every one of the earth's pores. Some of us fall asleep, head in hand and standing, leaning and sitting in the water. When we waken, it is some past noon the same day, and the tree frogs are trilling.

Pushing on, we discover the way is very treacherous, with drop-offs at every turn. The trail is too washed out to continue thenceforth, so, as the shades of evening descend, we take council on what to do. Peter advises that we try to breach the many falling rivers farther up where he has been scouting around and has, he says, found a safe crossing for donkeys, mules, and men. I glance at the grotesque wilderness of rock: Out of the jungle rise fantastic pyramids and cones of limestone, beyond which thick forests of gigantic trees make the awesome shapes of prehistoric monsters. Whatever god made this land was in terrible anguish when he left it half-finished. Such are my scribbled thoughts.

At eventide we come to the place of which Peter spoke—a web of tricky, trickling rivers all flowing into one great, misty marsh. Here it is necessary to proceed with the greatest of caution, for it is impossible to tell what depth, or even width, the main channel holds. All sides are barred from passage, especially with loaded animals. The footing is untrustworthy at every remove.

Our party moves on, slowly. We are like a wounded centipede, feeling its way, foot by foot, rippling over the watery grounds until we at last come to the main branch of the water flow, where I deem it necessary to go forward according to height, as that will tell the tale of how deep we are going to sink.

Hercules, being tallest, goes first. He is followed by Peter, who is shorter by only a few inches. They hold their weapons up over their heads with straightened arms. They make it to the opposite bank without incident. Then the rest of us follow, leading our mounts (if we have them), and the mules make it soberly and confidently and quietly across, but the brave little donkeys bray as if badly beaten.

I, being the shortest—many jokes are bandied on my account—bring up the rear, with Sneezer yipping his delight at the chance of a real swim; and he goes round and round the deep jade pool, yipping like a pup.

When I come to the middle of it, I find the water up to

my chin—forthwith my head goes under . . . somehow, I manage to keep my sword and my two pistols aloft of disaster. But, again, everyone gets some amusement at the expense of my poor height. I let them have their laugh and join in it, too, so as not to be a bad sport. (I know that I am the littlest leader that ever led men; I know that I am short as a stump; no matter, after the guffaws, they ask *me*—not Peter—"Where to, sir?") Respectfully, I, in turn, ask Peter the way. This is not kindness but prudence. Whereupon he points south and east. That way we go, lugging our tired, hurt bodies along in our soaking, squeaking boots and shoes.

Duggy says to me, "Meester Creengle, give up and tek off de boot dem." Whereupon, I give him my best smile and do so . . . I take off my waterlogged, heavy black boots. Now I'm barefoot like him . . . like all the Africans, who manage so well on the slippery rocks. Shared smiles on the faces of Duggy, Bulla, Barra, Pawnzo, and Hercules when they see me divest myself of my leathern load. (I tie my bootstraps together with a bit of vine given to me by Hercules and sling the boots over my shoulder.) Duggy laughs, says, "Watch me now—"

He's built like a muscle-legged rooster. The comparison serves him well, as he hops and jumps, sort of fluttery, from one rock to the next.

"How do you do that?" I ask him.

"What?" he says, standing on one leg, scratching his head. Would that I could move with so much freedom. Geechee, however, moves slowly, mincingly, staring vacantly out of those dark, haunted eyes; yet when he sees me bootless, his face cracks into a smile.

No one rides anymore—it's too roughish. Toward midnight, or a little thereafter, we take another rest; and from the hampers come some more goodly treats—sourdough bread and dried herring. Our thirst, too, is quenched from one of the many waterspouts that sprout naturally from the rocks.

"Come, Tom, look wha' me find," Peter whispers, while our group, after their feasting, is all adrowse and aslumber. I follow him high on a little path he himself has just made. A number of leagues from camp, he stops in a tiny clearing. There, on all sides of us (but for the solid mountain), we have a view of the country we have traversed, which in the milky moonlight stretches way far off to the distant coast.

Yet—it is the landscape below that holds the eye in a spell: There it is all jungled up. Towers of impressive gray rock soar upward. I gasp at the sight of it and say, "Peter, how can I write of this? Words cannot contain it. . . ."

Sneezer, hearing me exclaim such, sneezes. Then he barks once, quite loudly. Followed by echo barks throughout the stunned, still valley. Peter chuckles, lays his hand on my shoulder, says, eyes twinkling, "Dat don't stop you from drawin', Tom." To which I assent, as usual, to his good wisdom.

After this peaceful interlude, Peter and I drop back down to the little encampment where Hercules, Bulla, Barra, Pawnzo, and Geechee are at watch where I left them. Nothing is stirring anywhere except some far-off screech owls making their high, thin, tremulous cries.

"So, Tom," Peter says in that sage way of his, "yuh bethink it strange dat de ones watchin' are ones to be watched?" He means, by this, that the Africans are watching over the white men. I smile. True enough, they have taken over, in a way. Ever since our battle with Jenkins. But more than that, a kind of camaraderie has begun that befuddles my eye at times. For I have never seen the like, white men being so close and easy at elbow with slaves. Then Peter says what I'm thinking: "Dem free men, Tom. Slave no more."

"In their thinking, you mean?"

Peter nods. "Just so. Dem useful now. Not just fi labor. But fi doin' somethin' dem know."

"Which is?"

"Dem know dem can fight, Tom."

"Like any man pushed to his limits, I suppose. But they know how to make camp and break camp and how to move along quietly, and they seem more at ease here in these woods than any of the rest of us."

Peter grins. "On de ship, now, you haff de sea leg dem. Here inna de bush, Hercules and him men got de best land leg."

I get up from where I'm sitting against a rock and move a little closer to the fire. "If I were pressed to it, Peter, I would say that these men were equal to us as sailors, too. All in all, they conduct themselves as if in uniform, so that I wish, in truth, they really were."

Peter sighs. "Dat nuh be a bad idea, Tom."

"What?" I ask. "Putting them into uniform?"

"Twould free dem out of slavery."

I mull over this in the reflected light of the campfire, which Pawnzo has built up against the cliffside. I watch him roasting a breadfruit over the coals, his eyes also aglow. Not far away is Duggy, furtively slapping at mosquitoes.

Peter's right, of course, there's no way to justify this hideous system. But what am I to do? I have orders and I bear the king's decree to uphold them.

After a while I stretch out again, and the soft, lisping streamlets and the sobbing, soft owls slowly put me to sleep with my arms around Sneezer.

### *June 17, 1813*
### *On the way to Maroontown, sunrise*

When I wake, the sun is up burning off the fog. In a short while, we are munching on slices of roasted breadfruit and we are on the march, Peter piloting us up the slick, creviced rock toward the top of the mountain. Past the clearing where we tarried the night before, we find a broad field. There on the near hills are huts of wattle and daub and thatch. Also some red cattle and white goats on the level, grassy places.

People come out and stare at us, craning their necks to see who and what we are—their curiosity is considerably less than ours, however. Suddenly I am struck by the notion that, like it or not, I am a kind of slave trafficker, not unlike our nemesis, Mr. Jenkins. It is like this: Slave-trafficking is outlawed, and we, by definition, are transporting slaves . . . therefore, we are indeed traffickers, acting, in fact, against our very own law.

This being an inner dialogue, so to say, I tell myself that, *We are legal transporters, returning merchandise to its proper place. Proper? Place? Merchandise? Well, truth to tell, the proper place would be Africa. But are human beings property? Are they chattel? Are they wicker and wood?* But now we reach the juncture of the first road we have yet seen since we left Falmouth. But at the same time we see our proof of destination, three big men come out of the bushes—Maroons, they look to be, standing one chain ahead and taking deliberate aim at us with their muskets. We've got no alternative but to advance, which I do myself—Sneezer on one side of me, Peter on the other.

The two marksmen have a hard time deciding on who, or what, their target is—so they settle on me. As we walk toward them, Peter says, "Just face dem down, Tom." Well, perhaps we have no other choice than to march into the muzzles of their guns, but it is the most unnerving thing I have ever done. Those armed men stand seven feet tall, or so it seems to me.

When one of the long guns is pressing into my breastbone, I ease back a little. Then, in the clearest English I have yet heard in Jamaica, the armed man says, "We must stop you." To which—with my heart bumping wildly—I remark, "Captain Cuffee said he would watch over us and he has done so admirably, so let me introduce myself. I am First Lieutenant Thomas Cringle, and this is Pilot Peter Mangrove. My dog here is called Sneezer."

At this, the man smiles but it quickly fades.

Then, as this guard surveys the whole train of us, Cuffee himself comes through the bush all out of breath and says, "Let dem come ahead." And the other Maroon orders us to follow them.

We go along a very neat red-clay cart road that, very shortly, enters into a cross section. Presumably, as the direction is south and east, the intersecting road goes to Port Royal and Spanish Town, while the other, which we take, goes deeper into Maroontown. Built around a circle, the town is a scattered collection of wattle-and-daub houses, most of them thatch roofed and with an inner courtyard of scrubbed clay.

Soon the great Cudjoe comes up the walk and greets us. I experience a little leap of heart when I first see him. He is a presence to be reckoned with, a man on whom all eyes naturally rest. He is every bit as big as Hercules, but much leaner. However, as we stand before him, wondering what next to do, the weather turns round; the sky begins to lower, and it starts to rain. White, hard raindrops roll about like pearls on the reddish clay. Our men make exclamations of astonishment—and on closer inspection we see that it is not rain at all, but hail!

Cudjoe does little at first to shield himself. Then he takes a sheepskin that is scrolled up under his arm and, of a sudden, he unfurls it and throws it up over his head and shoulders. With all the ease in the world, he motions us to follow him—and we dodge the ringing bullets of hail without success, hopping and covering our heads with our hands.

On a path set off from the village we arrive at the skirt of the jungle again, into which, set solitary and tucked up, is Cudjoe's thatch house. On the left side of it is a field, which I think is young wheat. We are taken to a sort of barn—four posted with thatch over the top and no enclosing walls. Here we stable our animals, unburden them of their loads, and feed them bags of dry corn. After which Peter, Sneezer, Mr. Nedrick, Mr. Catwell, and myself repair to Cudjoe's conical house, behind which is a great outdoor kitchen, where a cheerful fire has been prepared. There, Hercules and company gather and are fed from a copious pot of stew.

We sit opposite Cudjoe, who lounges upon a leather

saddle that has, at each of the saddlebows, two holsters with pistols nuzzled inside. A little woman serves us each a tin cup of coffee with chicory, chocolate, and sugar in it. After we finish this, she gives each of us a calabash of fried eggs and hot peppers.

We devour every morsel, and the woman then brings us fricasseed wildfowl and roasted yam. Outside, the hail pounds down, turning the jungle to steamy blue islands. In spite of the storm, or because of it, the song of the tree frogs comes on, loud and strong. This steady music, combined with the feeling of warm, good food, makes us drowsy. However, when the last wishbone is plucked clean, Cudjoe gets right down to cases.

"I understand," says he, in his rich baritone, "that you have brought some people to me."

I cock my eye at him, seeking to catch his meaning.

Seeing my lack of comprehension, Cudjoe leans back in his saddle, his muscular calves thrust forward. After a spell of silence, he says, "I mean to say that when you British want cudjoemen to fetch up back your slaves, we do just as you wish."

"According to our mutual agreement, the treaty," I add.

"Yes," he concurs, "according to that which my ancestor, whose name was also Cudjoe, signed in 1738."

"Why do you say that we have brought people to you, when what we seek is really shelter?"

He smiles, and I feel that, somehow, I am in the presence of an ancient king of Africa. He certainly has that look about him, and it is in his wise, dark, wide-set eyes, and in his well-formed mouth, all of which give him a comely, calm, reasonable presence.

I will not deny that I quickly feel a fondness for him.

He continues: "We were slaves when our Spanish masters were defeated by you British in 1655. And, always, you British could not vanquish we, not with all of your militia and guns."

Cudjoe points with one forefinger to Sneezer, who is grinding down a hog bone at my side. "It took *them* to put us down," he comments dryly, "your dogs."

"Dogs?"

Cudjoe says, "When you bring slaves to me, it is different from when I bring them to you. Those that I bring, I render up to you. Those that you bring, you render up to me, for these are not runaways. This is an old unspoken custom, which is well known among you British . . . and we."

I must confess I do not like Cudjoe saying "you British" over and over—but why, I do not exactly know. Is it because, sometimes, I do not always feel that I am any more British than anything else? Is this what it means to be seen as a thing rather than a person? Is this what it means to have prejudice? If so, he is prejudiced against us British, and I am just another of the king's chessmen. That I have thoughts and feelings of my own, that my closest friend is an African, has not occurred to Cudjoe. Nor could I, in so many words, make him see who and what I am. For the first time, I believe I have an inkling of what it means to see through eyes other than my own.

Outside, away from the fire, the cold rain slants down. I say to Cudjoe, "My orders from Captain Smythe of the *Kraaken,* a ship of His Majesty's Royal Navy, are to return these men—who were stolen by pirates—back to Cinnamon Hill, where they live and work."

Cudjoe's black eyes, which rarely blink, bore deeply into mine. Mr. Nedrick coughs. Mr. Catwell sighs. Then, there is the sawing of Sneezer's teeth on the hog bone and the dense rattle of the rain. Peter is seated, cross-legged, on the other side of me. His inscrutable face betrays no sign of alarm—he remains as well composed as Cudjoe.

I am thinking—a foolish skirmish with the Maroons is not something any Navy man would wish to engender.

Cudjoe says softly after another silence, "We lose many men to you British; it is natural you give back some to we." Then he turns his head toward the barn and asks quizzically, "What do them say? Them wish to stay with us?"

I must confess, it never occurred to me to ask. But I answer him thus: "According to British law, these men are the property of Cinnamon Hill plantation."

However, even as I say this, the words go dry in my mouth.

"Why you did bring them here?" he demands, tightening his jaw.

"In order to evade the pirate, Jenkins, with whom we have had two dark encounters."

"So, to escape from that man, you must render up these men me. Fair?"

I have no answer. I can feel my men staring at me; I drop my eyes toward the fire and say carefully, "What would you have me do, Cudjoe? Must I break our law to keep yours?"

Cudjoe gives me an agreeable grin. "You must, sir. But first ask the men what them want—stay or go back to slavery."

Peter puts his hand on my shoulder. He whispers, "Him have we, Tom. And dere is Jenkins—him wait inna de jungle. We stuck 'twixt lion and tigah."

*Maroontown, evening*

As it turns out, this affair ends up being the darkest night of my life. First, there is neither moon nor stars, and the heavy clouds settle like moths on our heads and we are bedded down, with our donkeys and mules, and with the grumbles of thunder moiling amidst the hills in hoarse murmurs like the low tones of an organ.

In truth, I believe Cudjoe is right in what he says. Yet, what to do? In the light of a coconut oil lamp, I call the men together, mariners and Africans alike. I begin, "Men, we've lost nothing but, mayhap, we may yet have gained what we couldn't have foreseen." I look around at all the eyes that are upon me; their stares are deep. In the gold light, no one stirs, not one man. The far-off thunder grumbles, and I continue:

"Our enemy, Jenkins, awaits us. Where, we don't know, but surely he is out there, just as surely as thunder." And, at that moment, as if I had orchestrated it, a crack of light parts the darkened field outside our shelter, and then it is followed by a great, portentous thundercrash!

Mr. Nedrick tugs at his red sideburns. "I say, Mr. Cringle, we be beggin' you to cut to the chase. . . ." He adds pertly, "Before the fox doubles back and catches up with the hounds."

A general chuckle from everyone.

"Very well," say I, "the long and short of it is that Cudjoe wishes us to leave behind the men of Cinnamon Hill."

"The slaves of Cinnamon Hill," Mr. Catwell corrects.

"As you wish," I sigh.

Hercules, who is squatting on his hams, says forcefully, "You mean *we?* You mean *we slaves?*"

"Are we *free,* Meester Creengle?" asks big-bellied Pawnzo, standing in the straw by himself.

Peter looks at me. "Mek we say somethin', Tom."

Relieved, I give him the go-ahead.

Peter gets up. He is a long figure of scrawniness and he casts a tall, dark shadow on the straw. "Mr. Cudjoe," he starts off, "him a shrewd mon. Him say, what come fi him, stay wid him. Him say, what go, nuh stay. Understood?"

The lantern-lit men look at one another, shrug and nod, but no one says anything. I am feeling just at this moment that I would like to be anywhere but here in this damnable position of decision maker and leader.

A white owl on a post by the edge of the wheat field

hoots once, then chitters and dives for something . . . I cannot help visioning my friend Obediah. He and the owl came to visit me when I was sick at Cinnamon Hill. And, for this reason, it's comforting to me to see an owl; it gives me a feeling of strength.

"So," Peter concludes, stroking his bearded chin. "If oonoo want fi stay inna dis place—den, stay wid Cudjoe. De rest of we move way on de morrow. . . ."

Mr. Catwell, leaning against one of the four stationary poles that hold up the thatch, is picking his teeth with a straw. Lifting his hand, he catches my eye. "What I want to know, sir, is how we come to bring men, as is owned by Cinnamon Hill estates, to such a forsaken place as this—while, mind you, riskin' our lives in the lee of it?"

"That," I reply sharply, "is for Providence to decide, for not even King George—if he were here among us—could imagine that such a place as this exists, and given that it does, that it is owned by anyone such as Cudjoe. It is all a mystery—no less so than slavery itself. Why men should risk their lives and lose their lives to harvest sugar, for which they do not even get a taste, is beyond my ken."

My ringing words in the eerie night surprise me. It is, I own, a larger voice than the man that used it. I look to the fence pole and see that the owl has returned. After this little speech of mine, no one says a mumbling word, and all is deathly still except for the pulsations of thunder.

I stay awake scribbling this down. The truth is, I fear not to fight but rather to do wrong. And the thing called slavery cannot, in any way, be rightful or supportable, here or anywhere on Earth.

I feel Peter's hand on my shoulder. I look up from my notes. He is smiling and singing this little song:

*"Tom, Tom, come up*
*From rivers of water.*
*Tom, Tom, come up fi breathe*
*Freedom from slaughter.*
*Tom, Tom, de beat of a drum;*
*Tom, Tom, de heart of a mon."*

We sleep the night in the hay of Cudjoe's stable, warm in the cold air of the Cockpit Country. I lie therein listening to my heartbeat, my head resting on Sneezer's flank, my arm touching Peter's arm.

*June 18, 1813*
*Back through the bush called Look Behind*

This morning all are in agreement to go back—not the way we have come, but overland across the island and to the south, making our course down toward Bluefields Bay, where a year ago we were swamped by the rogue wave that crushed the *Bream* and drowned all the crew but Captain Smythe, Peter Mangrove, me—and, the devil take him, Jenkins.

This is pretty safe passage and mostly free from marauders. However, we do pass little wayside villages with poetical names like Quick Step, Burnt Hill, and Barbecue. Thence, out of the mountains to Alligator Pond. From there to the southeast and Bluefields Bay—there to seek out a ship that will transport us round the point to Port Royal.

Peter tells me that the Africans who wish to stay at Maroontown are those shy men, Picky, Maubie, and Mafeena. Those who want to go back to Falmouth are Geechee, Duggy, Barra, Bulla, Pawnzo, and Hercules. I am grateful the ones coming along are fighting men, worth their weight in gold bullion. And the ones staying behind are not only less known to me, but even reserved and quiet within their own ranks.

As to the reason *why* the men want to be with us, I have but a small clue. Perhaps they have family back at Cinnamon Hill. But also, I sense they feel some spirit of adventure with us—some furtherance of a plan that may lead to something good for them. I don't rightly know, but I believe their desire to bear arms against a notable enemy, with whom the score has not yet been settled, is the chief reason they've linked up with us! Anyway, there is no telling what these men have suffered under the hand of Jenkins. The three who remain behind I confess to not knowing. Perhaps they did not want to be known to me—certainly they held back from it. But, in any event, they seem quite resolved in their intention of staying.

As for Mr. Jenkins, I do not expect he'll follow us across the Land of Look Behind, for it's the most precarious place on the island of Jamaica. The bush called Look Behind is equally ominous in name. They call it I-No-Call-You-You-No-Come—and for good reason, I am told. There are poison

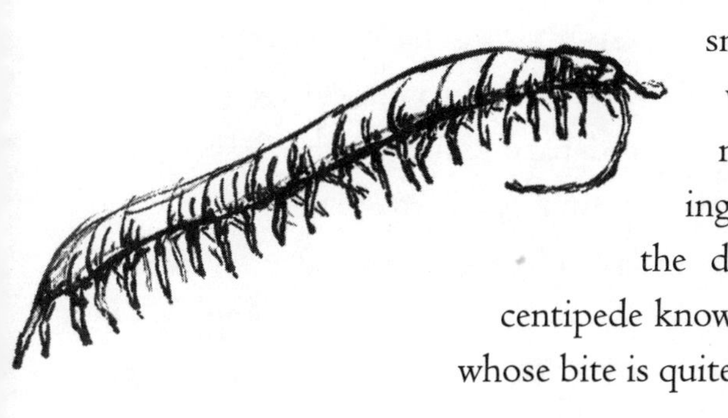

snakes and ferocious wild hogs and all manner of crawling, biting insects, like the dreaded eleven-inch centipede known as a forty-legger, whose bite is quite deadly.

*Later that day in the Land of Look Behind*

So it is that we say our multiple good-byes to the new Maroon conscripts, and we venture forth into the wild bush. Cudjoe and his Maroon infantry sound the abeng at our departure and give us a touch on the heart. That is to say, they, each and all, touch their own heart with their right fist as we march off into the unknown.

I must say that I am not without concern for my own welfare—if and when we get back to civilization. For the Africans we've divested ourselves of at a current value of three thousand a head in shillings are the lost property of the Cranston plantation. And even as I do what conscience requires of me, I realize that I am no less an outlaw than Jenkins. In point of fact, I stand but a yardarm from my enemy in the matter of the law's noose.

So off we go—and me a-scribbling—into the fiercest tree-shadowed gloom that any man has ever seen; a veritable green hell it is, and the light leaking through its pores seems like the shafts of sun seen underwater on the reef.

I write this on the back of my donkey, scritching and scratching, up and down.

*Hellfire noon of the same day*

After quite a long haul, we lie down in a little clearing, full of the mixed emotions of our departure. The farther we go away from Maroontown, the less we seem to go *anywhere.*

I feel we are adrift in a tidal flow of leaves. Once, descending into a chasm's an awful noise—grunting and stomping.

Peter fires his gun, and out of the growth come a herd of wild rooting hogs, huge old, tusky snouters, heads low and nasty—but none try to attack us. Needless to say, they startle our stock. Their squeals and thunder make for mayhem, and we fall over ourselves trying to get out of the way.

Then, too, the harsh music of parrots follows us everywhere we go. And this is accompanied by the fitful tramp of feet and the swipe of cutlasses as the thickish creepers are cleared for passage. After much unmitigated walking we take our rest again, too tired to go another step. We drink our fill from a streamlet. Then, after appointing watch, I drop off asleep and stay that way until I am startled from a dismal dream—

Once again, it is Jenkins who haunts me. In the dream his face is pressed to mine as we tumble in a death grip, his fingers grasping for my neck and mine seeking his—only to come awake, all hot at the throat. Just a little distance from me, there raises the head of a monstrous serpent, which is gazing earnestly upon me, his mouth slightly parted, his tongue tasting the air. Is it a dream? Or am I awake? I am so much alarmed that I tell myself that I am still a dream.

I imagine it is the old Serpent Himself, the Devil, preparing to close my account. I want to shout out my consternation, but all that comes from my throat is the croak of a crow.

Sneezer, sleeping right by my head, starts up all alert and ready for a fight. Peter comes quick, cutlass in hand, and with him half a dozen musketed men, but *all* they see is *me,* writhing and contorting, as if wrestling with some unknown adversary.

Now Sneezer begins to bark, and I am on my feet screaming, "Snake, snake!" Nedrick, Catwell, Hercules, and Peter give the bush a good thrashing. All the while, unperturbed, my satin visitor lies low, grinning at me from a branch of logwood until he slides gracefully through the leafy litter and is gone without anyone else seeing him.

This is the worst thing, too. That no one but me lays eyes on him. "Peter, his body is the . . . size of a . . . man's," I stammer.

And it was—is—I swear on my father's headstone.

But since no one has seen the serpent, no one will vouch for its existence, and everyone eyes me queerly, making me feel that we are sadly alone with our immutable perceptions . . . real or not real does not matter one whit . . . all that holds true is what we *think* we've seen—or what others confirm as undeniable.

The snake leaves me feeling quite uncertain of myself. So I, too, ask myself—was it really there? Or was the thing a phantasm of my imagination? My conscience is split on the matter—whether true or false, let devil or angel decide. This prickly moment Hercules comes over to me and says in a confiding tone, "Mr. Creengle, sah."

"Yes, Hercules."

He gives me a half smile and then he nods over at Barra, who gives me a knowing look. "Both of we," Hercules continues, "know dat snake be real."

"*How* do you know?"

"Me smell him."

I am really puzzled by this—but pleased, as well, that someone should take my side. Still, I do wonder what a snake smells like, for I have never been introduced to one in that way. I ask Hercules what sort of odor does a snake give off. Barra answers, grinning, with his low-slung bottom jaw slightly ajar. "Dem smell *raw,* like rotten egg."

I sniff the air for some sort of sulfury odor, but there's nothing there I can detect.

We travel on all the rest of this night, occasionally stopping to rest and refresh ourselves with some hard biscuit and a draft of water from a freshet, but as daylight approaches we climb slowly up out of the valley, and, by morning, we are on the summit of a high hill, and there we see a sight that no one will forget.

The hard, blue line of the far blue sea drawn cleanly against the decisive margin of the forest. A bit of blue, like a band of hope that sends us tramping on, unbreakfasted but undaunted, down into the next valley . . . and up into the next . . . ad nauseam, but always that hint of the sea to calm our nerves and leave us greatly expectant.

*June 19, 1813*
*At the edge of the world, looking down upon day's end on the south coast of Jamaica*

We come at last to the other side of the island. We know not for certainty *where* we are, but we are satisfied to have come this far unmet by any disaster.

So, for the time being we stop and make a cooking camp, and whilst Hercules and company are preparing victuals, Peter, Sneezer, and I climb a green stone spire well draped with vines, and all we have to do is haul ourselves up, walking the while, as if we were born to walk at such an odd, vertical angle to the earth.

As we ascend, Sneezer looks up from below, his head and body growing smaller as we pull ourselves to the top of the rock.

Atop—which turns out to be no taller than a topmast—we see well over the vast expanse of the jungle. The view is not anything but what we'd thought it would be: a beach of sand hard-pressed by the circling arm of the cerulean sea. A delicious sight it is.

I doubt whether any discoverer of worlds feels more joy than Peter and I at this moment, and we can hardly refrain from uttering a vain little shout to celebrate the end of our wanderings.

So we gaze on that berm of blue with the shoreline gilt in gold and the sun going down most glorious and glad, and in this suspended moment of fantasy, I see the white owl of two nights before—could it be?—seeming to follow me, and reminding me of Obed once again.

After a little while, we lower ourselves down from this eminence, and bit by bit, more careful than we went up, we arrive on terra firma, and the first thing I notice is that Sneezer is not there to greet us.

"Him prob'ly chase way dat snake," Peter chuckles.

But I think otherwise. "Something's wrong, Peter, I can feel it."

So we start off back to camp full of worries—at least I do. There, we are rewarded with horror and chagrin: We find a broken camp with men gone, donkeys gone, food spilled everywhere, and no one in sight anywhere.

Worst of all, for me, is Sneezer being gone.

Peter calls me to a spot of ground where there is a small hill of spilled gunpowder. "Dem tek everyting," he says, "but dis."

"Looks as if someone, trying to reload, spilled powder—"

"Dere's blood, Tom. Look, a whole heap of blood."

We study the telltale spots of darkish blood, already drawing flies. Once more I feel I have failed in my duties as an officer. I shouldn't have left camp. Now I will pay the price for being absent. "Well," say I, "there's nothing to do but go after them."

Peter casts me a leery look, then, shaking his head, he sighs and says, "Dat wha' dem want we fi do. Look, over here."

He stoops down, and on the brownish, damp leaf litter there is another torn shred of bandanna tied to a thick hank of curly black dog's hair. I pick it up. Then pitch it away with a shriek, for the thing is soaked with blood.

Peter says, "Get hold yourself, Tom." Right now my head is aching and my heart is down in my throat, but Peter reaffirms, "Dem want we fi follow—so we nuh do dat. We go down fi de sea instead."

"Down to the sea?"

"Dem 'ave a boat dis side, Tom." Peter's eyes gleam.

"How do you know, Peter?"

"Dem 'ave a boat, both sides de island."

"How do you *know*," I repeat obstinately.

He shrugs. "Me just know, mon."

"Well, friend," I tell him. "I trust you better than myself, so whatever you say goes. And if you say they are going to the coast to meet a ship, I believe you. How we waylay them is another thing—that isn't written yet."

"Tom—you goin' fi write it!"

***June 21, 1813***
***On the south coast, midnight***

Well past the midnight watch, Peter rouses me to waken, and we leave our hiding place under the weeping withes of a giant willow tree. There, swatting mosquitoes, we have spent the bitter hours of the day gone by.

On the shore, a moon-filled fog prevails.

"What we need," say I, "is a good, concealing fog."

The ocean lies still—not a sail or a crest to whiten its gleamy surface.

A peculiar feeling, this. We are in retreat, yet also in pursuit. We have lost our mission, yet we're trying to regain it. We are alone and somewhat lost, yet all round us there are clusters of huts set up on the shore. We come to a flat place of stunted, twisted trees. These stand thorn-ridden in the fog moon. All around us knotty cactus plants grow and we stay between them, walking in the soft, still-warm sand. Barefoot, we have slung our boots over our shoulders opposite our muskets. And so, very determined, we press on into this unfamiliar territory; my previous gladness at having reached the sea has turned to despair, as I have lost the thing dearest to my heart—Sneezer.

On top of that, I have sacrificed my command, my men, my very soul on this agonizing coast.

What constantly comes to mind is this: But a year gone by, I was challenged to be the first mate and pilot of Obediah Glasgow. Kidnapped, I ended up his friend. We fought side by side—it is still hard for me to believe—against my own Navy!

If such a thing could turn out all right . . . then what of this? Might not this come round, too?

So that now, as I trudge across the copper sand, I hear Obed's voice, so true and clear, and as if he were there with me:

*Your soul will never be a stranger to mine,* he told me.

Well, Obed, if you are anywhere near, look down on your poor friend now. Then I remember him saying a little riddle in that broguish way of his: *If Right is Wrong, and Wrong is Right, then where does Truth sit tonight?*

As we look on the sea, the first thing to meet our gaze is a sailboat with a silver sail directing her course near to shore. This, like everything else, seems an act of Providence, and Peter motions me to drop down behind a dune overlooking the beach, where he says, "Wind blowin' from de shore."

"Then that little boat is beating against the wind."

"Favorable for we." He winks, showing me that old indomitable spirit of his. "What we haffa do, Tom, is rush 'pon her bow."

A little discussion of how this is to be done follows.

When the clouds cover the moon, he says that he will make a run for the boat while I swim within reach of her. Before this, however, I am to shoot down the helmsman. If he is brought down quickly, even before Peter gets there, the craft will luff in to shore and she will be ours. Then Peter strips down to his trousers. I examine my musket, and seeing that it is well loaded and primed, I peep over the dune and watch him run fast for the curling tide.

I have no desire to kill someone in the sharpie way of Mr. Nedrick—all concealed like this, with the poor man so unsuspecting and in the clear, an open target—yet, what choice? Thus do I take aim, holding my breath and squinting tight my left eye.

As Peter swims close to the boat, I squeeze the trigger and feel the musket buck against my shoulder. Down drops the helmsman and up jumps Peter, and a scuffle ensues, telling me that my shot is inaccurate, and that the man is barely scratched; and this I know by the way Peter struggles against him.

At last, I watch Peter raise his fist and deliver a knockout blow, and the boatman crumples. Then Peter throws him into the sea. The boat luffs up in the wind, comes near to shore. Whereupon I run with Peter's clothes, our ammunition bag, and our muskets. I get across the sand and out into the shallow surf, where Peter greets me.

No time is lost in shoving her about and getting her bows away from the land, and there is now a fresh breeze from the shore and Peter has the sails filled. Soon we are under a brisk headway, free upon the sea in a craft of our own.

Under the rust moon I see the bobbing head of the man Peter has scuffled with . . . he is swimming into shallow surf, fumbling for the beach. Attending to the sail, Peter says, "You crease him, Tom, but him a big fella. Me haffa knock him out again and trow him over. But him strong."

"I thought maybe he was bulletproof."

"No, you parted his hair," Peter chuckles, "but dat only mek him angry wid me."

In the clean, fresh, seagoing breeze, we feel animated by our success, for at last there is a sail over us and we are slapping along, making rapid progress and rounding the point. I find a bag of provisions shoved into the point of the prow, so going steady ahead with the good wind, we eat our first meal at sea—and a very good one it is, indeed. There is jerk pork, very salty and spicy. We munch it down, all of it, licking our fingers. Here I think of Sneezer and how he would love the bones, and that makes the water come to my eyes.

Peter, the master pilot, is at home. "Look," he says, pointing north, "ain't dat a schooner, mon?"

I glance where he gestures and, sure enough, I do see something hard against the dawning light.

"Dat mon me tump, him a scout. Look dere . . ."

He stabs his finger past the peninsula we are rounding, and there it is—a ship!—just as Peter says. I am wondering, though, how the two of us could possibly overtake her. The sails of our boat—a tiny jib with a sort of homemade sail—are full of breeze. But how, pray tell, does a skimpy little jib overcome a great corvette?

Peter, seeing to the sail, which is rippling and popping, tells me, "From de moment me eye see him, me know we board him."

"That's what has me vexed, Peter; what do we do *after* we board her?"

Peter grins. "Oh, dat." He shrugs. We both watch the huge ship—no great distance from the land—cut her course up the south coast.

Peter taps my shoulder. "I leave dat fi your glory, Tom."

"My glory? What is that?"

He ties the sail down where the wind has flapped a corner loose. "Me job is pilot."

"Yes, that is true. And you are the best there is."

"Your job, Tom, is fi get onboard an' free de men—and mek we nuh fergit Sneezer."

I chuckle at this, his confidence in me. Here we are in a delicate little sailboat without even a swivel gun. The corvette ahead of us will be hugely armed, and I have not a clue how we are going to overtake her, much less overcome her. Yet if Peter thinks we can, I shall try to think so myself, and once again I remember Obed's words: *My soul will never be a stranger to yours.* And I also remember my small prayer sent upward.

***Somewhere near Lucea, in Cornwall Parish***

The chase is over, or so it seems, for we have pulled up way past the midnight watch and well into the morn and we are within scudding distance, some twenty chains away, from the ship named the *Flora,* whose deceitful flag, I notice, is Spanish.

We are not at war with Spain, but this war with America drags on, and these beggars play tricks with flags and run up a different one whenever they like. It is with no great urging on Peter's part that I am elected to swim the distance between our mooring and theirs.

We are in a cove, and Peter's argument goes thus: "Get to de ship, quick-quick, an' me will distract all-a-dem on shore." It is a plan and one that should gain us flattery in Port Royal—should we pull it off without a hitch—but there is one large problem.

"How do you expect me to free our men from the chains that surely bind them in the hold when the upper deck is undoubtedly well guarded by Jenkins's pirates?"

"No, sah," Peter says, cocking his head and smiling, "dem no get lockup."

"Why do you think not?"

"Pirate know dem fear fi shark and just stay put onboard."

He rests his eyes on the *Flora* and continues to smile, and I say to him, "Shouldn't I fear for sharks as well, Peter?" The clear waters lap crisply underneath our little craft, and but for our proximity to the shore and the small island separating us, we would stand out and be seen, yet as it is, we are under the cover of palms, well concealed.

"Shark nuh trouble de strong, Tom."

"What about Tim?"

"Dat water haff blood in it—dat bwai were swimmin' inna blood."

"All right," I relent. "Give me fifteen minutes to get over there, another fifteen to find Sneezer and our men. Then, you make it seem as if there is an army ashore, and we'll make our break and swim for this island."

Peter promises to make a hullabaloo in the bush, as if the schooner is under attack and he has a fat bag of gunpowder and shot, and he knows how to make a bamboo cannon . . . so, this is our ungodly gambit. I am set for my swim, wearing shirt, trousers, floppy felt hat—but no shoes or any other weapon other than the knife on my belt.

And so I slip into the calm, warmish water of the cove and prepare to strike out for the *Flora.* One last look back at Peter, and I go off into the sea cove.

Of all the dangers to which I have been exposed, this is

indeed the most nerve-racking. Whilst I employ my usual sidestroke, moving easily through the water, I see—flashing before my face—the anguished eyes of Tim as the shark lugs him away forever. My agitation is so great that I wonder why I do not sink from the weight of it. Truly, every time I throw my feet for a hard kick, every time I employ a stroke of my arm, I fancy the smiling mouth of the turned-up monster that grabbed Tim and shook him like a doll. Try as I might to ward off the memory, the horror of it keeps sliding back.

But here there is no sign of an offending fin. Just the unrippling cove, clear in the moonset night. And as I draw near to the *Flora*'s side and I imagine the danger is quite past, I hear a familiar bark. Getting closer, I see—of all things!—a boarding ladder hanging down into a dinghy that floats alongside the bow.

Suddenly, my nervousness overcomes me, and I have a near fit of shaking. Then I hang, half in and half out of the water. What better incentive for a shark to bite me in two?

Unable just yet to pull myself up, I grip the ladder and try to overcome the shakes. Finally, I take command of myself and heave my quaking body over the gunwale and into the hull. There, I find myself amidst a great pile of fish heads.

I give myself a moment's rest, then resume my attack up the bow of the *Flora* by the ladder provided for such purpose. (Apparently, someone is about to use the dinghy, for it is set up just so.)

Anyway, hand over hand, I ascend until I reach the top, where I discover that Sneezer is tied to an iron ring about two chains aft.

All hands are asleep. No one is on deck that I can see. Yet no sooner do I imagine that the *Flora*'s crew is in a rummed-up stupor, safe in their hammocks, than I hear voices coming from the fo'c'sle, and so I lie flat, listening to the voices fall and fade as distance robs them of their volume.

Sneezer makes not a sound, but I see his eyes on me and his tail wagging furiously. Except for the steady bump of that tail, the night is now still but for the intermittent chop of the outgoing tide. Taking a deep draw of air and exhaling it slowly, I recover a sufficient degree of boldness to pursue my mission. But I must say that my heart is hurting, it is beating so loud and hard.

I stand up—or try to—unsuccessfully, for now I discover I cannot move. Something is pinning me to the deck. Am I turned to jelly from fear? Can I not stand?

No, I feel underneath my shirt and find that I am really sticking fast. (If you do not know ships, you will be surprised to learn that the heat of the day brings the pitch in the seams up to bleed, and this is the reason I am stuck like a barnacle.)

Anyway, I can't move for the pitch without tearing my shirt and trousers asunder. Well, it is either *that*—or be captured! So, I roll one way, then the other. By using all my strength, I, at length, tear myself from the deck. My shredded shirt and a piece of my trousers fall away.

I am such a sight—but no matter, duty is duty. Naked or dead, I pursue my task. So, I now run toward the forward hatchway, where Sneezer is tied, and in a trice, I unfasten him and he is all over me, sneezing.

I hug him hard, and he pushes me down, and then something plucks me into the air and I am caught by a gigantic hand—"Mek a move an' me snap yuh troat," says a familiar voice, and who should it be but Hercules—and behind him, Bulla, Geechee, Duggy, Barra, Pawnzo, Nedrick, and Catwell!

Too good to be true, but truth is self-evident—it was *they* who had tendered the dinghy and were setting things up to make their escape before the rise of the sun. Without further ado, we hasten to it and start down the ladder—everyone, that is, but Sneezer and me. As soon as they are within the dinghy, pushed up together like peas in a pod, I shove Sneezer overboard and dive in after him.

As I make the surface, someone who has heard the splash calls out from above, "Who goes?"

Mr. Nedrick grins and clasps me on the shoulder. "You're a sight, sahr," he whispers, "nekked as a well-oiled rat." His teeth shine in the night.

"Nonetheless, living . . . ," I tell him.

However, same time, I hear Peter's unlikely bamboo cannon burst a round on the lee side of the *Flora,* and so our attacker ducks down, giving us a second's remove to shove off.

"Have you any weapons?" I ask Mr. Nedrick as I squeeze into the dinghy the men have readied for their escape.

He replies, "Has a tick got hounds, laddie?" I see he has his long rifle, as does Mr. Catwell and the Africans. Mr. Nedrick is taking aim before we even round the *Flora*'s mermaided bow.

"To the island, then," say I, and all heave to, with some plying the water with their hands. Hercules, aft, breaks off the rudder and uses it for a paddle. Soon the overloaded little ark is moving toward the island.

The tide is ebbing fast, which means that (just as Peter thought) the *Flora* will be stranded for a time. But now the cove is shallow enough to walk in to shore, and the men jump free of the dinghy and make a run for it.

Meanwhile, Peter's barrage is like Admiral's Boxing Day. He's positively raising havoc aboard the *Flora*. She is firing back, in due course, with eighteen-pounders that pummel the shoreline and send up fountains of sand and frond. Parrots are screaming, and the moment Sneezer sets foot on shore, he starts barking madly.

Hastening to make good our escape, we run a good ways south of the firing line and find a well-used pig path and take it full speed to wherever it may lead. Running all out, I trip on a root and go down face first, just as an iron ball meant for my head strikes Geechee squarely between the shoulders. He drops dead onto the pig path. I check his breath and feel his stopped heart—he is gone.

"Mr. Creengle," I hear Hercules say at my ear. I get up amidst more thumping of the ship's cannon and cracks from their sharpshooters. We go farther away from the beach, deeper and deeper into the mangrove bush. The silence from

Peter's quarter tells me that either he is running after us—or he has been captured. I hope for the former.

*Somewhere off Lucea Point at noon*

Peter appears, limping cumbrously, some moments later. Ahead, there is a clear space abeam of us, all full of sun-bleached shells and green land crabs, and as we come up the crabs shrink back into their warrens. Peter's face is flecked with ash. His eyes dart about.

"Where Geechee?" Peter asks, gasping.

"Him gone," Hercules replies gravely, shaking his head.

I feel this death worse than Mercy's, for although it is strange to say, I felt communion with this vacant-eyed man, whose spirit somehow touched mine more than once. And now I have three deaths weighing heavily on my conscience, and more, I am afraid, to come.

"How did you make that cannon bark like iron, laddie?" Mr. Nedrick queries, trying to relieve the sudden silence of our beleaguered little group.

Begrimed, Peter grins, his teeth flashing. He gets to his feet. "An old trick me learn from Mr. Horatio Nelson inna Cadiz. True, dem bamboo cannon sound crisp and real!"

"Is that how you got so mucked up in the face, Peter?" Mr. Nedrick asks.

"Me fire from swampside, dat way dem have nothin' but trouble following me track . . . anyhow, one of dem bamboo dem blow up in me face."

Despite the severity of the situation, everyone laughs—and Sneezer barks, and I have to clamp his snout shut with my hand for fear he will alert Jenkins to our whereabouts. The shelling is stopped, but we can hear a great amount of yelling back by the cove. No doubt, they are already after us.

"Are they hot in pursuit?" Mr. Catwell asks, getting off the log he is sitting on.

Peter nods. "Me tek dem deep into dat bog, dem be busy wid dat fi while."

"I suggest," Mr. Nedrick puts in while looking at me, "that we make a move landward. I am not greatly fond of this crab country."

Peter snorts. "Dis all crab-lands straight fi Montego Bay."

"What do you recommend, then?" I ask him.

"Me think we hide inna de Milk River, den go upland a ways. Where de river get narrow, dere be a marl road dat go north. Mek we follow dat."

"An *open* road? How do we know Jenkins won't be laying for us?" I ask.

Peter's eyes narrow. "Him will, Tom. Him be wherever him want fi be. We must ready fi him."

Mr. Nedrick, wiping his reddish wool whiskers, says, "Well, laddie, if that be the size of it, we better be off now."

"Me don' like dis," Pawnzo gripes, lugging his pudgy bulk forward. Short-legged Duggy, named after a rooster, is always on the move, nervously darting his head about, and he wastes no time now. They are followed by Barra, and close on his heels, Bulla. Hercules doesn't bother to run—yet his feet seem to roll under him, and, leisurely or not, he gets there with everybody else by some amazing force of will.

Thus, helter-skelter, we go through the thickets of the

mangroves, led by Peter, who swings his wooden leg out to the side, grabbing my shoulder to steady himself from time to time. Finally, we come to a river, which has the bluey pale color of goat's milk. Here we are all on the lookout for snouts of crocs, but aside for one huge beast sleeping on the tulle bank in the sun, we see no such, and continue on well after nightfall, when the crickets and frogs raise up their rackety roar.

Under the protection of a great silk-cotton tree, with a partially burned-out trunk into which we all fit, we take our first rest.

Taking stock of our situation, I order that there is to be no thought of food or fire. Peter, however, quickly finds us a decent little spring for drinking; that, sadly, is to be our only sustenance.

Here we are clustered about the snaky roots of the silk-cotton tree, hunched down for a bit of mosquito-pestered sleep, but at least—for the moment, anyway—we are not being chased.

I am off to one side, writing.

Peter is at my starboard, head resting on his hand.

Sneezer, whose broad back I am using as a kind of desk, is lying down at my feet; I am cross-legged beside him. Every so often there comes the loud, unfriendly grawk of a heron. Occasionally, too, the boom of a crocodile—some male making known his territory.

Writing is too difficult . . . after a spell of it, my mind refuses to work. I drift, sleeping on and off, pen in hand. Fitfully, I dream again of Jenkins. His fire-scarred face flashes before me. I waken with a start.

Sneezer is growling. He shifts his position, curling himself closer to me. Every joint in my body is aching, and my neck is red-hot where my unattended wound is. Altogether, I am one great tense bundle of crouched suffering. But then I am quite sure that everyone feels the same. Again, I am reminded of Obed—this infernal swamp with the grawks and belches of unknown birds and beasts brings back that night on the Cuban coast when I tried to save his neck. . . . This, somehow, reminds me of Tim—I push his face away from my thoughts because he, in turn, reminds me of Johnny, my first messmate. Then come the phantom faces of Geechee and Mercy, each dead under my command . . . I try to push them out of my thoughts.

Then I hear the call of an owl off in the mossy, shrouded night, and for a moment the owl's hooting is Obed saying, *Your soul . . . will never . . . be a stranger to mine. . . . Your soul . . . will never . . .*, over and over. I imagine him looking down on me from the ghosted trees.

Sneezer interrupts this soft interlude with a low, grating growl. He crouches, rigid as wood. One great bark, and everyone is awake. Guns clank, hammers click as men stumble to their feet.

"What goes, laddie?" Mr. Nedrick asks.

My heart jumps as I feel something evil in the swamp, something near. Sneezer, meanwhile, is no way fearful, but continues to set himself into a fit of sneezes and barks. I can scarcely hold him back.

"Let 'im go, Tom," Peter says, so I do.

Sneezer makes an exaggerated leap into the darkness. I

hear his forepaws strike water, then all the earth seems to move and a scabrous mud log is before me. I see the white of its open mouth; it's a twelve-foot croc whose foul breath reeks of the rank swamp.

Sneezer vaults behind the croc, snapping at its lashing tail.

"Him too close to de dog, me cyaan get off a shot!" Hercules says.

Neither can I, since I am so backed up against the tree.

I step into the muck, pistol cocked and pointed, yet the croc's head cranks too quickly. Then the lash of its scaly tail clumps a violent spray of black mud into my eyes.

I wipe them clean with my hand, and while I'm doing so, Mr. Nedrick steps forward and thrusts his long gun into the croc's cottony mouth. Then comes a blow of meaty thunder, and the very bats in the boughs of our tree charge off on leather wings, beating the humid air, filling it with squeaks.

The croc, mortally wounded, goes into a series of convulsions. Sneezer dances to and fro all the while, and then Peter does a coup de grâce that kicks the beast backward. Big Hercules and bantam Barra both start pounding him with their gun stocks. The croc upturns his white belly to the moon and rolls once more, and floats away, looking exactly like a rotten log.

Round and round the hammocky swamp there is a bat-shuddering displeasure, as if the very foul soul of the place had been irretrievably disturbed.

The distant heron rookeries begin to cry and wail. Peter, shaking his head, says, "Jenkins know where we be now."

"Then we're gone, laddie," Mr. Nedrick remarks.

Gathering up our arms, we slink off into the gloom.

Sneezer limps beside me, having been struck, I think, by the croc's cast-iron tail. There is nothing to do about it, though, for, looking behind us, I see torches coming . . . Jenkins is right after us.

We hear, in due time, the coarse voices of his pirates, too.

But as if this were not enough, Bulla is bitten by a scorpion while resting against a big tree. So now we have to stop and tend to Bulla's bitten face—he is stung on the nose. It is hard to see anything, for the trees are so thick, but Bulla's nose—believe it or not—is visible even in the darkness, and it is already swollen as large as a fist.

Bush doctor Peter administers to it as well as, if not better than, Mr. Jigmaree. He plops a handful of wet mud over the nose and a good deal over Bulla's face, too. Into his mouth he puts a hollow reed so that Bulla can breathe while the mud covers his face completely.

This thing is performed in the dark whilst the noises of the oncoming pirates bear down as their torches light up the moss and mangrove night with an almost dreamy fairy's light.

Bulla, now equipped with the muddy countenance of a snapping turtle, whistles breezily through his reed and waves his arms to say he is all right. So we trudge onward with the swamp birds constantly crying at our invasion.

Finally, we reach high ground, and it is then—as Jenkins's men catch us slowing down—that a small scuffle breaks out in the rear of our line.

Turning, I hear someone scream—it is not one of ours but one of theirs, apparently. A crunch of skull bone is followed by a splash and the quenching of a torch—all of which tells me someone's down.

By the time I get there with Sneezer and Peter, there's a pirate with a truncheon facing off some of our men. Right off, he is checked by Sneezer, who rips his loose-fitting trousers down to his knees.

At that, despite the seriousness of it all, we let out a great laugh. The pirate drops his cutlass to cover himself, and Hercules comes up close and drives his gun butt deeply into the man's middle. Down goes the swine, gibbering senselessly.

Before the rest of the rascals catch up, we head back the way we came. Some minutes after, we are out of the swamp for good and up onto the moon-white marl road, and we run as hard and as fast as we are capable; in back of us, Jenkins is shouting, "Shoot, you idiots!"

They have caught up with our rearward guard again, I imagine, but then I see their pitchy torches dimming in the depth of the swamp, so that it appears they are retreating.

"It Bulla," Peter tells me when he hears the story from Duggy.

Up clomps Bulla with his grotesque mudface and his reedy nose and his eyes bright white, and the rest of his face so cracked and ugly, I know full well what has happened: Bulla has scared the torchlights out our pursuers' hands. It humors me to think of it, for pirates are among the most superstitious people and swamps are the most fearful of places (known to be the haunts of duppies and hants), and the effect of Bulla's face must have been horrific, to say the least.

Just imagine: Out of the darkness comes this crack-faced, lump-nosed monster with a whistling reed mouth.

No wonder the pirates scrambled when they saw him.

The small edge it has given us counts for something, and we use this advantage to get farther down the road.

### *June 22, 1813*
### *On the way to Montego Bay, midnight until morning*

The rest of this night we continue with our fast-paced run, taking but one rest beside a little roadside spring. The water is so cold, it makes my head ache. I soak my kerchief and tie it round my sore neck. My arm, thankfully, has not troubled me at all.

And now the darkness is going gray, night is fading. My white owl calls to me from a cliff. At this point I cannot but believe that he is a sign from my old friend. Anyway, it is comforting to me to think so. As yet—no sound that we are being followed. We head on through the dawn fog that scatters at our feet as we go.

At first light, we come to a little valley with an abandoned Great House in very bad repair sitting on a sort of knoll. Behind it is a small, sturdy-looking stone church.

"Now, there's a stout place to hold them off," I tell Peter. He agrees.

I give the order and we load up and head for the little church. It sits, safe and strong, just up from a frothing stream of water.

No sooner in than we hear the boom of a gun. Jenkins and his men have just gotten into the Great House, and they're firing at us from the open windows.

Within the chapel there's an ancient air of sanctity and silence. I look through a shattered window casement. The pirates are all at their perches looking down the barrels of their long guns.

"Heads down, laddies, they're mounting their attack," Mr. Nedrick cries.

A bullet chips the wood frame of the open door. Then a bang, and a chunk of shot chips the stone behind my head.

"It's time, Mr. Creengle, sahr, for a counterattack."

"With much dispatch," urges Mr. Catwell.

"Have we dry powder?" I ask.

"Enough to powder their noses," Mr. Catwell replies.

They're now throwing shot at the tiny cathedral; the walls are ringing with chips of stone.

Sneezer gives a great, doleful howl, followed by an abrupt sneeze.

Pressed to the cold, clammy floor, the whole crew of us looks at Sneezer, and laughs. Then I unroll my hasty battle plan whilst Sneezer crowds up against me and outside a downpour of rain adds to the steady song of whining lead.

Says Mr. Catwell, "Well, we may be half drowned, but as long as Hercules is here, we'll keep the ears about our heads!" True, Hercules is a trump in any battle.

But before I can make them know my plan, Mr. Nedrick gets up and peers out the north casement, and cries, "Now, laddies, quick upon it, ready yourselves for the worstest of attacks!"

The hammer of his long gun clicks.

"No time, Mr. Creengle."

I jump up to see a hardy half dozen tumble out in attack formation. They stop, uncertain, at the river, which they'll have to cross to get to us, there being a little humpback bridge just in front of our main door.

The thing, as I see it, is that they won't chance the bridge. They'll be forced to ford the stream. To get at us, they'll swim—which means presenting their heads as targets to our marksmen. This much Mr. Nedrick has already surmised and is, indeed, acting upon.

*Moments later, at our battle stations . . .*

The wretches come so fast, I haven't time to get my pistols primed. Yet I believe the chapel will hold them off—if only we can hurl enough lead in their direction. One casement to the east, two to the north, both of which offer ample views of the oncoming ruffians.

The muskets are quickly divided amongst Mr. Nedrick, Mr. Catwell, Hercules, and myself. Bulla, Duggy, Barra, and Pawnzo have pistols.

Sure enough, one of the pirates pushes a floating barrel ahead of him into the stream. He disappears before we can get at him.

"There he is," I cry, "just below the bridge."

Mr. Nedrick squeezes off a shot, but the blackguard ducks behind the barrel.

Another pirate, crossing the stream, uses a log to hide himself, but Mr. Nedrick fires between the dead branches and wings him. "That's a hit," he hisses triumphantly.

He asks for a loaded gun. I hand him one, and he says to me, "Sahr, see to it I'm well covered now."

Then he unbolts the front door and, flashing forward, opens fire on a third pirate, who's making a direct rush for the bridge.

At the same time, the pirate behind the barrel rises up with another volley—this aimed at Mr. Nedrick.

Mr. Catwell fires on him, the barrel skids loose, the pirate sinks.

My ears ring from the explosion of his gun.

Mr. Nedrick backs in, lodges the door, and bolts it. "Another took care of," he says proudly. "How'd you fare?"

"I pierced the barrel a bit," answers Mr. Catwell.

"Better look again," I tell him. "He's still hanging on."

But the moment I say it, he slips under—a dead floater.

For the moment, then—with two down—they slacken their fire.

The chapel's full of smoke.

Three booming flashes from outside, very near, behind a patch of trees.

"Dem mount anudder attack," Peter shouts. He goes to the window, aims, squeezes—the smoke-and-boom is followed by silence.

"Did you hit your man?" I ask.

"Me don' tink so." Then, aiming his head up yonder, into the tiny bell tower of the chapel, he asks me if I think I could fit up there.

"No one but me could even try." I hand him a reload gun.

"From dere," Peter says, "yuh 'ave good sight of dem on dis side."

Yes, if I can squirrel my way up there while the pirates are all deployed at the windows, I might be able to pick a few off.

So, I use the ledgy stones of the wall to climb up the tall tower. I've one long gun in hand, two pistols jammed into my belt. Once up into the little tower, I'm able to see all in every direction. However, there's no room to fire a long gun. So I drop it back down, stock first, to Peter. He tosses me up an extra pistol, and I now have three of them.

From the tower I see the man who's been pelting at Peter; and down by the stream the rest of the pirates are beginning to spread out for their big rush. I spot Jenkins. The tail of his stocking cap's sunk in the water. He's pushing a floating log in front of him. At either end of it are two more armed assassins. But the worst thing—there's a brass swivel cannon mounted on the log.

Then the villain close to Peter makes a run for the chapel. Before I can hit him, he reaches the open window and fires into it.

Mr. Catwell yells, "I'm hit!"

"Bad?"

"Not murderous bad, but bad enough," coughs Mr. Catwell.

I see that he's hard on his rear, feet splayed out, trying to hold himself up.

The one who shot Mr. Catwell is off to the side. He's almost on Peter, who doesn't see him.

I point and fire, and drop the man in his tracks.

"Good shot, laddie!" Mr. Nedrick crows.

"Me owe you, Tom," Peter says.

"I take no pride in a lucky shot," I say, but it's a lie. I'm proud of it, all right. At the same time, I pray Mr. Catwell will live to see the morrow.

For a moment the firing from outside stops as the pirates watch their dead comrade float downstream.

From my perch, I say, "They're coming, the three with cannon."

"Can you peck them? I dinna know how to get round that far side," says Mr. Nedrick.

"I'll try."

Down below, Peter's tearing a piece of shirt to make a bandage for Mr. Catwell.

"Hercules, can you make that wail of yours?" I ask.

He replies, "Why you want me fi do dat?"

"I want you to give them something to think about while I shoot down on them."

"Me give yuh de lion's roar, mon."

"Burst outside," I tell him. "Peter, you cover him. Oh, oh. Two are coming up on us!"

Hercules throws open the door, wailing like a banshee. All pirate eyes upon him. Same time, I fire on Jenkins. My shot strikes the swivel gun, making it ring. The force of my bullet rolls the log and drenches the deadly little cannon.

Furious, Jenkins calls out, "Charge!"

Another man on the bridge—Hercules shoots him, gets back in, and bolts the door.

As I'm now known to be in the tower, a blizzard of shots are thrown my way. I drop down into the chapel.

"Come, Hercules, let's rush them."

Throwing open the door, he drops to one knee and shoots at the men coming up from the river.

Sneezer is barking at my heels. I lunge toward the bank, firing at Jenkins's midsection.

Bullets spank the water in front of me.

Jenkins, untouched by my shot, spins the log round to knock me down.

I dive into the river, swim underwater, straight for him!

When I rise, he's right before me, unhurt. We lick into each other, grasping at throats. Mine burns like fire. Sneezer paddles up and bites Jenkins's cap. This catches the man off-balance, pulling him backward. Jenkins writhes free of my throat-hold then. He comes forward, jabbing with his knife.

Ducking the blade, I receive a ringing blow from his bunched left fist.

Everything goes black.

When I come to, it's with the feeling that someone—or *something*—is pulling me up. Sneezer—I think. Yet when I break the surface, I see he's gnashing at two others.

Jenkins grabs my shirt and drags me toward him. I'm all floppy. I slide weakly toward his knife—then, a miracle!

As I'm about to merge with Jenkins's dagger, something underneath the water pulls him down.

He vanishes.

Sneezer's still fighting.

What's under there?

Jenkins's head comes up. Startled, eyes bulging, he drops down again.

In his place, another face pops up.

Is this a dream?

Off to one side, Jenkins is afloat.

"He'll live," Obed tells me.

I cannot believe my eyes.

"What is it?" he asks. "Are you so surprised to see an old friend?"

It's his voice, all right.

"You're . . . alive."

Obed grins wide. Those are his straight, white teeth, all right.

"Seems Tommy's a bit under the weather, and not made of the mettle he once was." His voice is soothing, teasing.

"You didn't . . . die?"

"Tommy Cringle"—he laughs—"well, you saved my neck a time or two, about time I saved yours."

Obed steps up to higher ground, and I see we have floated a ways downstream, the current taking us, swirling and swimming, down into the mangroves. We're marooned on a plump little island of mangrove trees. Sneezer paddles up.

Obed grins and says, "Just like old times."

Sneezer sneezes, gives his fur a shake. Bits and pieces of bark fly everywhere. Then he gives a big, heaving sneeze.

Jenkins floats past us. Obed and I catch him by the collar and drag him up to the front of the Great House. There, Obed flashes me another grand smile and throws his strong arm around my neck.

"Ah, Tommy," he says, sighing, "it were worth the price on my head to see you—even under such wettish conditions as these, eh?"

"What *price?*" say I. "There is none. The Royal Navy believes you dead—as have I this year gone by."

"Oh, a wanted man is ever a wanted man," he says chidingly.

So here is the real, flesh-and-blood Obediah Glasgow, standing there in his soaking wet grandee's shirt and his sopping pants, and he looks every bit the man I piloted for on Cuba's unlucky coast. I admit to myself, he is the father I had always dreamed of having after my own was lost at sea.

"So, it really was you—alive and well and not a duppy—on the windowsill. You know, when I was raving mad from fever."

Obed grins. His locks are tied back, but his squarish features are framed by their bulge behind his head.

"Should I have told you the truth, then? Or go on and let you think whatever you would? If you'd known I was alive, Tommy, would you have loved me just the same? Ah, but you're the patriot and I'm the pirate. We both know that, full well, and there's nothing to do about it."

"Just tell me one thing?"

"Anything."

"How did you not drown? You were manacled and chained."

Obed laughs hard at this, saying, "Have you never heard

of a creature called the *Armondillo?* A curious beast, to be sure. Has armor on't, from head to foot, and when the little beast encounters a spate of water, he don't attempt to swim it. He walks upon the bottom till he reaches dry land."

"And . . . *you* . . . did that?"

"I had a good lungful of air before I purposefully let go your helping hands, Tommy. I sunk out of sight; everyone assumed me dead. Then I just walked to a little floating island. When I got up top again, I drank the air like rum!"

"Obed, you're alive!"

"Aye, that I am, Tommy."

"I still can't get over it . . . and how you saved my life."

Obed says, looking over his shoulder, "You've seen nothing of me, Tommy."

"I'm glad to say I have . . . and then I haven't."

He grins and gives me a parting hug.

"That man Jenkins, I only knocked him out. If you fetch him back up to Port Royal, you'll get some shillings for his hide, dead or alive. Catch him while he's still blowing bubbles—and do look for me soon, lad, in Port Royal, for I've

a bit of a proposition to make you, a business deal, so to put it."

He starts to slosh downhill toward the old sugarhouse and the underwater marl road. He stops, waves.

"Tommy, your soul will never be a stranger to mine," he calls as he goes into the mangrove trees, and vanishes as he came. I hear him sloshing and fading off, going to his freedom and to his exile.

Then I cast my eyes down to Jenkins, still oblivious.

Sneezer has his mouth on him—should he awake.

There are no more shots coming from the other side of the Great House, and seeing Peter come round the side, smiling, I know we have won the day.

*June 27, 1813*
*Aboard the Flora, South Coast Bay*

It seems I am in good stead again.

How so, the luck of it, I may never know. But, no doubt, Providence and good fortune have conspired to see me through the thick and thin adventures of this young life of mine.

Mayhap, I am blessed by Obediah Glasgow, who may be—who can know for sure?—my true-life angel. Long have I felt the presence of his soul so near to mine—only to find out, in the end, that it was not his spirit but his real person watching over me.

How a pirate—one so worthless in the world's eye—could mean so much to me is not something that I, an officer in His Majesty's Royal Navy, am prepared to resolve. Yet that is the truth of it: Obed is the pirate, and I am the patriot, though I may be a little bit of both myself, now and then.

However, it is enough to know that Obed's eyes watch over me like my own father in heaven; not to mention those other loved ones—Sneezer, and earnest Peter Mangrove, ever my companion-at-arms. For all, I am humbly thankful to be alive.

That said, or writ, we sail on to better climes and lesser woes—or so I hope.

I'm captain proviso of the *Flora,* which, along with Jenkins's Falmouth-anchored ship, the *Hornet,* I shall get a share of, as shall all who shared in the overtaking, from His Majesty. It is the honor due us and the wage paid us for risking our lives—to answer Mr. Catwell's question some days back in the Cockpits.

The monetary loss of slaves to the Maroons will be balanced out—if need be—against my reward money for the capture of Jenkins.

So onward, up the coast. We bowl along before the breeze, and I do my best to overcome the gloom that clutches my heart, and think only of positive things, like the fact that Mr. Catwell is recovering nicely from his wound. And the fact that Obed lives! Often I think of how he must have followed Jenkins's actions and, pirate to pirate, known of them in the most intimate fashion. That is the only explainable way he could have shown up as he did, because he was so close on his heels, and ours.

Always on my mind, like a constant wind from off the coast, is Obed's promise that I'll see him again . . . somewhere soon in Port Royal. This has me peeking over my shoulder, I can tell you.

Just now, a sharp, digging motion of the *Flora* tears me

away from my scribblings. We begin to pitch through a head sea, close set upon the wind, and there is that old familiar tumbly feeling that I remember so well from my first days as a midshipman, starting out as a frailish, fearful cabin boy, dreaming of his father's noble profession.

### *June 28, 1813*
### *On the Flora, Port Royal Harbor*

For all of yesterday the good breeze that luffed us off finally failed us. Thenceforth, we either stormed or lay becalmed, flat as a ducat. At midday we lay roasting in the sun until dusk, when the current—not the wind—garnished our complaint with a little forward bubbling.

Presently, the wind picked up, grew lusty as before, and we made some steady, measured progress. For supper we ate red snapper that was hauled onboard by Hercules and Barra. (Bulla, by the way, is still nursing his nose in a pumpkin paste made up in a mortar by Peter.)

I'm inclined, today, to feel much less the worse about my moral dilemma. Safe haven has done it, mayhap, and the encouraging sight of Captain Smythe, whose ship greets us with the rising sun. We catch him coming round the point after he picked up the captured-and-weighted-with-stone corvette, the *Hornet.*

"I am so happy to see you alive," he roars, "that I could clap and sing."

We are on the deck of the *Flora* when he says this, with both of our booty ships in port.

How joyous it is to lay eyes on Captain Smythe's great,

good grin. In the privacy of my quarters, I convey to him my long tale of woe, the ultimate loss of the Cranstons' slaves, the recapture of the rest, the battle with Jenkins, and his eventual defeat and hang-up in irons aboard the *Flora*.

I have my eyes fastened on his the whole time I am talking to see how he assesses my wantonness, my progress, my good spirit or bad.

"Why, Tom," he roars at the end, "you princely little coney—have no worries on any account. The latest broadside from home has run a long diatribe about how the West Indian landlords will have to change up their affairs if they are to stay in business."

He punctuates this with a gob of spit out my open window.

"As you well know," he continues, smacking his lips, "we have more trouble on the horizon, heat and smoke enough, without this, but the long and short of it is that there's now brewing a scheme for the gradual abolition of slavery! Can you believe it?"

I feel a prickle on the back of my collar, goose pimples all along my spine. So, it has come to this . . . much sooner than we expected!

I ask, "How does that excuse *me,* sir? I mean, with the loss of so many Africans—two who died at the hands of Jenkins's muskets, and three who defected to Cudjoe."

Captain Smythe claps me the back, and as I am not expecting it, he almost knocks me down. Which causes Sneezer to sneeze and me to cough, and Peter, who's standing by, to laugh, and Captain Smythe to say, "Tom, you still don't get it, do you? It will soon be *law*—each slave shall pay off his value, according to his power to pay installments, which is a new term they are throwing around town. The planter may be put to inconvenience, certainly, but to little else, for he shall have his justly compensation. And there's an end to the whole bloody business."

I must say, it's a bit hard to bridle my confusion. Seeing this, Captain Smythe pipes up again: "Look, I know an easier way round all this! Let's just conscript these brave souls, these Africans who have so loyally served you—what do you say?"

"Is that warrantable . . . legal?"

"Indeed."

"Well," I say, so much relieved, "if it's good with them, it's great with me!"

"There is the matter of the Cranston estate," Captain Smythe rejoins, "but it can be gotten round, especially if we throw them some coin."

"I cannot imagine how that old purse-face Mr. Cranston will take it."

To this, he takes a snort of snuff, shrugs, and says, "As well-nigh law, I hope." Then he adds, "After accounts are settled—you'll be a rich lad."

So, my heart is considerably lightened to know this. Now there is but one unfinished business: squaring things away with Mr. Cranston.

### *July 1, 1813*
### *Port Royal Barracks*

A visit to the Navy surgeon, who tells me my arm's all right; my neck scarred but otherwise fine. The little scar over my right eye, quips he, "befits an officer of your tall standing."

"But I'm sitting," I say.

He grins, chuckles a bit.

So, to a hot bath at Navy Hospital, and—how about this!—my first shave (though I needn't have bothered, there being so little furze to nick off), and after these painless ablutions, Peter and I give Sneezer a bath.

I must say, I liked my damping-down a lot more than he does!

Then the three of us stroll down the white, powdery noon streets of Port Royal, with me looking around all the time for the unexpected. Yet this comes from Sneezer rather than Obed. Sneezer takes a sour turn in some clover of the horse, as they say, and this abruptly ends my first day ashore—with another bath for Sneezer, after which we're too tired to indulge in anything further.

### *July 2, 1813*
### *The Hound and Horn Tavern*

I, Tom Cringle, the little lieutenant, am no longer so down in the mouth. . . . Here's the reason why.

Captain Smythe, on clearing two ships through the naval purser's account book, is given the kingly sum of one thousand pounds for each ship. This to be divided in equal shares among the crew. My share comes to two hundred forty pounds, plus the reward of capturing Jenkins, which is another five hundred pounds!

Grand news, indeed, but then Captain Smythe confers the best words of all: "Tom," says he as we are taking the harbor view by the bronze statue of the martyrs and the sun is splashing down on our heads, "I am the bearer of even finer tidings—not only are you the richest young man to stride on Port Royal's promenade, but I am given to understand that because of your outstanding service, you are now going to make captain and hold command of your own ship, the *Flora*."

I am, once more, bowled over backward by this revelation. Peter, good soul, just chuckles and says, "Me tol' you so, Tom."

Suddenly I am beside myself with joy: a captain, a ship of my own!—and, on top of it, a trip, betimes, to old England with a merchant cargo under my convoy of no less than a half million pounds' worth of goods!

All this has transpired in just a few honorable hours. Suffice to say, it is the happiest day of my life—that is, until I have lunch with Mr. Cranston at the Hound and Horn on the Junction Road outside of Half Way Tree, and there I am so nervous that my hands start to tremble like the proverbial bishop on All Hallows' Eve; and why, I wonder, in the single blessedness of the hour, do I fret so unnecessarily? It is all shillings and pounds, is it not?

Mr. Cranston, with his pompous wig resting on his knee, vaguely stirs the turtle soup tureen and asks me, "Do you find the port agreeable, Mr. Cringle?"

Confound me—I cannot be certain if he alludes to the harbor port or the Madeira port that he is drinking. He is that way—vague as the nor'west moon in a fog.

Clearing my throat, I say, "I find all ports agreeable, sir, when the mind's at rest."

"Well said. And the fish? Is that dependent upon the mind or the belly, sir?"

Now, at least, I know he is addressing the victuals, although he looks everywhere, all round, and never locks eyes with me.

"Have you considered my offer?" I ask. (I have generously, I think, promised some recompense for the losses of Cinnamon Hill plantation, and quite frankly, it is *not* something I *had* to do, yet something I *wanted* to do.)

"I have—and so has our new proprietor, Mr. Yardley," replies Mr. Cranston, taking another sip of the Madeira and smacking his lips with satisfaction.

"Is my offer deucedly *less* than what was expected, sir?" I'm having trouble chewing a morsel of sherry-basted turtle—tastes like boot leather to me—and I'm little by little scuttling it under the table to Sneezer, who, as you might expect, is tucked up at my boot heels sneezing down every bite.

"Not at all," answers Mr. Cranston crisply. "It is as fair as the expression 'What has been must be.' So, I am indebted to you, Mr. Cringle. For, as you know, this new law being conjured at home will upend the whole hogshead, if you gather my meaning."

I nod just as Sneezer snatches some turtle meat off my hand, accidentally nipping me in the process. Giving a little upward jerk of my head, I am studied by Mr. Cranston.

"Slavery, sir," Mr. Cranston continues, fork-wrestling with his own turtle, "is the wrong thing, and thank Jupiter, the fusty old Parliament is finally trying to settle the matter. I shouldn't be surprised if, on the morrow, we find the whole untidy affair swept away . . . and no one remembering why it was instituted in the first place."

He rolls his eyes and snorts voluminously, just as Sneezer sneezes under the table.

"Paid labor, Mr. Cringle, paid labor! Nothing could be simpler, or fairer—heavens, we make so tidy a profit anyhow. But do you not think our slaves should have their own lands if they wish? I have been saying all these years, whatever benefits *them,* benefits all. That's what I always say."

I stare at him in surprise. Of all the mealymouthed remarks . . . and I wonder what Peter would say, or Obed. I can hear Obed throwing back his head and laughing outrageously—*He runs with the fox and then with the hounds!*

Back on the hot, sun-dazzled streets, dizzy from the heavy meal, Sneezer and I are walking toward the harbor when a smallish old woman, wrapped in a black shawl, scrapes her finger along my arm and beckons me into an unsavory-looking alley. No doubt she is selling something, and also, no doubt, something I have no need of. Yet when we get back into the shady fastness of the leaning buildings, and Sneezer, oddly enough, seems so at ease with this stranger—in fact, he wags his tail expectantly the whole time, as if the old crone were going to feed him on something better than turtle—I am taken aback . . . and all the more so when the crone straightens up and throws off her dark cowl.

By God, it is none other than Obediah!

My heart gives a leap to see his sparkling face, and I color like a red-inked octopus wondering what he's doing in this, of all places, so heavily trod by uniformed men.

"Well, Tommy," he intones musically, "word's got round that you've been upped again, with a ship all to your own command."

I nod and grimace at the same time. "Obed," say I, "what's to become of you? You're in a kettle of well-stirred fish here, I warrant."

"Yet the kettle's not set to boil, lad. It's just of a pleasant simmer."

At this he cackles, not like himself but like the old woman he mimes—and a fine job he does of it, too.

"There, there, Sneezer old salt, give me a kiss of promise, won't you?" At which my dog's all over him, pawing on his shoulders, washing his face with a dolloping tongue.

Then he straightens himself a bit, and his face grows serious. "I've a proposition for you, Tommy, as I said."

I shift from one foot to the other. "I'm a captain now," I all but apologize, "and it's to *my* ship I would go."

"Are you above and beyond hauling a box of salvage from the sea?" he asks, winking and readjusting his shawl around his shoulders and head . . . for just then a lounging lot of sailors comes slouching by, singing like drunken larks. Before my eye, Obed stoops to about four foot and conjures himself so small and insignificant that even his massive shoulders pinch together and his square chin falls forward into his neck.

"Is it legal to do so, Obed?" ask I, watching the men scuff past out of earshot, blind to all but their merriment.

"As honest as pigeon pie," he answers, laughing into his fist. "Don't worry, Tommy, I'll not tarnish your brass buttons. I'll set the thing up so that it's as legal as a longboat on a sinking cruiser."

In spite of myself, I cannot help but smile at how complete his disguise is.

"So what's it to be, all legal and such?" I ask.

He replies, "There's a little matter of salvage out of Discovery Bay, a Spanish frigate from way back two hundred years. She's in lovely water clear as gin. All we've got to do is fetch the booty and lay her up in a safe hull for a little while. Now, you're captain of a fine seagoing vessel; I shouldn't think there'd be a problem, would there, lad? You just tarry awhile before putting into port, is all. And then wait for the sign of the white owl."

"But why a military ship, Obed? Why not one of your scrounged-up barks—surely you have one or two at your disposal somewhere?"

He blinks and winks and pats me on the shoulder, and sort of shoves me along as he edges us back into the cart-creaking street. Even with the daylight full upon us, he seems no more and no less than what he appears: a withered, back-bent hag on her way to market with a basket.

"My client," Obed says conspiratorially, "happens to be a man of your identical cloth. But let's leave it at that—you'll have all the protection you need, and you'll be hearing from me, Tommy, you can lay to that." So saying, he slips off and filters in among the plaid and cotton outfits milling about the outer edge of the open-air market.

ఆ

Well, when all's said and done—my times on the main being both good and bad—I have to thank Providence for life and limb and for seasoning of the good with the bad and not the other way around. I'm alive, doing what I do best—staying alive!

And so my tale is told, my yarn ended.

If I were to spin it longer, it would bend, end for end. But I wonder . . . during my boisterous and unsettled times, during lee currents, hard gales, foul blows, and swampings—have these things scathed and scalded my heart, and made me callous?

Peter insists, "Tom, you *tink* too much."

I reply, "Yes, but at least I *don't* think of *Tom.*"

Whereupon he chuckles, "Tom is de best horse to bet on. Look how him win de race—and him not yet fifteen years!"

"Well, Peter, have you ever heard this verse: 'I have shot mine arrow o'er the house, and hurt my brother'? I hope it doesn't apply to me!"

"No, Tom," Peter says. "You will be remembered as de one who set his brother free."

"If that is so, then my logbook and I have been around for a good reason. Someone may yet learn from our errors."

"I don' know what you love more, Tom, dat dog or dat log of yours. But a hunnerd years from now, who gonna kere 'bout either? Every likkle ting gonna one day pass away."

I hope—for once—Peter is wrong. I hope that long after I am gone, there will be a buoyancy in some of these words

I've written. I hope that some may still be afloat, but if not, I will gladly settle for what I have at hand: namely, Sneezer and Peter and Obed and the open sea, and some new adventures before the compass and behind the wheel. And—oh, yes—these are good enough for the likes of me.